The old rancher jumped to his feet, his chair falling back and hitting the floor with a bang loud enough to cause Lizzy to stir fitfully from her bed by the fire. "There was nothing to find you damned fool!" He pounded a frustrated fist on the table. "And I was afraid. Just like good old Jim, I was afraid of whatever was in that water. I was strong enough to stand there and call his name until my throat was raw and my face burned by the sun, but I couldn't bring myself to go any nearer to those cursed shadows that day or any other." A sob suddenly rocked the old man's body and he turned away in shame.

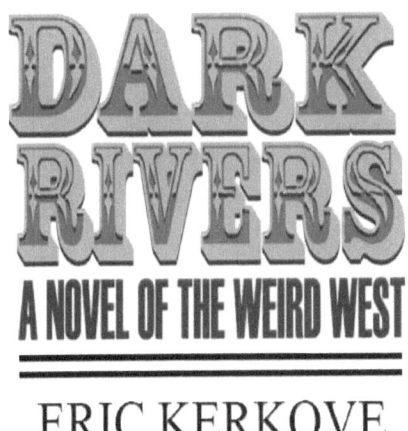

DARK RIVERS
A NOVEL OF THE WEIRD WEST

ERIC KERKOVE

Pink Skunk Productions, Ltd.
©2014

This book is a work of fiction. Names, characters, places, and incidents are products of the author's imagination or are used fictitiously. Any resemblance to actual events, locals, or persons, living or dead, is coincidental.

If you purchased this book without a cover, I would very much like to know where you got ahold of your copy. There aren't that many out there and if someone not only sold theirs, but also ripped the cover off first, it's a darn shame. Regardless, I hope you enjoy your purchase.

Pink Skunk Productions, Ltd.
Osage, Iowa, United States of America

ISBN-13: 978-0615973333
ISBN-10: 0615973337

Printed In the United States of America

First Edition: February 2014

For Craig,
A true cowboy in all the best ways.

Acknowledgements

I'd like to take this time to express my gratitude to Scott Lufkin, Marc Bergman, and Amy Moody-Qualls (Patron Saint of lost commas), all three of whom were kind enough to slog through the original manuscripts and help me to get the writing into its current form. If you find any errors within these pages, I assure you that they exist only because of my ability to thwart the efforts of even the most dedicated editors. I'd also like to thank Melanie Hoffner for her years of encouragement with regards to any and all of my creative endeavors, never really allowing me to believe that I couldn't do what I set out to do. Finally, I wish to express my gratitude for all of my friends and family who have always accepted and encouraged me despite the many bizarre twists and turns my life has taken There are probably still a few more left.

DARK RIVERS

A Novel of the Weird West

Prologue

Precious moisture had begun to bead and trickle down the cowboy's neck well before he had even reached the saloon doors. The barkeep, sleeveless undershirt stained with sweat and saturated with the odor of stale smoke and cheap liquor, watched the stranger with a dull expression while he pulled out a short, filmy glass and began to wipe out the inside with a rag too filthy to do more than smear the grime around. His blank expression brightened a little, however, when the cowboy slapped a scuffed silver coin upon the warped and cracking boards of the counter top.

"What'll you have, stranger?" the bartender asked from beneath a shaggy salt-and-pepper mustache.

"As much clean water as a nickel will buy," the cowboy replied while he hitched up the waist of his worn-out britches. "I've got me a *mean* thirst today." He plopped a battered canteen next to the nickel with a hollow clang. "And I've run my reserves as dry as the day is long."

"Can't help you there," the barkeep stated flatly as he set down the glass he'd been cleaning. His plump sweaty body settled into a posture of impatience. "I got shit whisky and I got passable whisky. Take your pick or take to the road. I don't need another body warming this place unless it's buying something I got to sell." He waved his thick, calloused fingers at the few scattered tables that filled the sparse room as if the two old men playing cards in the corner constituted a raucous crowd that he was eager to get back to managing.

The cowboy pushed the brim of his hat up with a battered knuckle. "S'that right?" He reflected quietly before hitching at his pants again and beginning his argument. "You saying to me that you're so hard up for the wet stuff that you won't take hard cash for one man's ration? Horse shit! Only way you'd be outta water's if the well went dry. If that was true you wouldn't have no people nor horses outside. I saw a couple of both and I'd wager they ain't as thirsty as I am."

The man behind the counter began to feel uncomfortably warm in a way that had nothing to do with the weather. He ran a nervous hand across his balding head as he eyed the well-worn gun belt the cowboy had strapped around his lean hips. "Believe what you want stranger. I ain't got nothing for you so you'd best be on your way."

The nervous man's hands dropped behind the counter and the cowboy figured that in a few seconds he would have a rifle in his face if he didn't heed the suggestion. The stranger figured he could draw and fire before the barkeep could get a nerve-rattled grip on his own weapon, but that kind of trouble wouldn't put water down his throat, although it might earn him a rope around it. "If that's the way you want it." The cowboy shrugged as he snatched up his nickel and still-empty canteen. "I'm sure somebody's willing to part with a drop or two if I'm willing to pay."

The bartender snorted. "Not likely stranger. You'd best just head on out of town and forget you ever found this place." Under his breath he added, "I wish I could."

The cowboy, already half-way through the swinging double doors, was about to turn and ask what the man meant by that when he felt a tug at his belt. Looking down, he saw a girl of no more than eight years looking up at him fearfully. The speed with which she'd come upon him made it likely that she had been waiting nearby for the stranger to exit. "What can I do for you, little lady?" the cowpoke asked through courteous but unsmiling lips.

"My pa wants to talk with you," she replied, taking a step back from the stern looking stranger.

"Well then why can't I hear him talking?" he replied, his insistent thirst adding an edge of impatience to his voice.

"He's out back, behind the saloon. He don't want old Albert seeing him with you," the child explained.

"Albert? That the barkeep's name?"

The little girl nodded, shifting impatiently in her thin, dusty sundress. "Come on," she ordered, running barefoot across the street and into the alley between the tavern and an empty barbershop. The cowboy stood for a moment and wondered if it was worth wasting any more time in such an unfriendly place. If he couldn't find water there, he'd have a half-day's ride to the nearest creek he knew of, and he wasn't getting any less thirsty playing games with local children.

"Ah, what the hell," he muttered under his breath as he made his way between the buildings. *Could be her pa wants to sell me some water but don't want that Albert fella coming down on him for it,* the cowboy thought. It was something to hope for anyway.

A stringy looking man in overalls and tattered work boots stood shirtless and nervous in the shade of the saloon. His skin was an angry red color, no doubt from many thankless hours spent toiling under the merciless sun. "Don't worry stranger," he said as the cowboy came into his view, "Al won't hear us back here. There's a room in between the bar and the outside."

"I ain't worried," the other man replied. "Where'd that little girl go?"

"I sent Lizzy home. I don't like her being back here," he paused and whispered, "It ain't safe. I figured maybe you could do something about that."

"Bout what?" he asked suspiciously.

"About the well," the girl's pa replied.

"I don't follow you," the cowboy said. "Look, if you've got water to sell, I've got money to buy it with. Ain't nothing else I got to offer."

"You got that," the thin man stated as he pointed a black-rimmed fingernail at the pearl handle of the stranger's weapon. "You know how to use it?"

"When I need to," the stranger frowned and placed a hand protectively over the holster. "I ain't killing nobody for no water if that's what you're thinking." He made ready to turn away when the other man spoke up again.

"My name's Ezra James, and I ain't no killer neither. And I don't wanna make nobody else one. What I *do* want is for somebody to take care of the well," he turned and gestured towards a large wooden crate with a pile of bricks on top. "And ain't nobody in this town want to do nothing about it no more. Whatever's in it makes the water like poison. Three people died with blood coming outa their backsides not long after drinking it, including my poor sweet wife." He paused a moment and cleared his throat, "A man from town, Sam was his name, thought it might be some kind of animal died down there and ventured in with a pitch fork to scoop out the rotting sonofa bitch. He ain't never come out, though. That was two days ago. I'd go down myself, but I ain't no tougher than the last fella and I ain't leaving Lizzy no orphan. No, Sir! But another week like this one and like as not we'll have to leave all this behind or stay and die of thirst."

The cowboy nodded his head and raised an eyebrow appraisingly. "What do you want from me?" he inquired.

"If you can go down there and clear up this problem for us," Ezra licked his cracked parched lips, "you can have all the water you and your pony can carry. Hell, you can even bed down at my place tonight."

"Why all the secrets?" the cowboy asked, though his thoughts were drifting towards the cool streams of heavy, dark water running beneath his feet. "Why don't you want Albert to know?"

"Cuz he don't trust nobody and he don't want no stranger messing with his well. He said it's just some oil's leaked into the stream and he'd take care of it himself but he ain't done nothin'." Ezra looked disgusted as he spoke. "It ain't no oil in the water's making people die that way, I tell you what. Ain't no oil makes a man disappear, neither. Albert's not doing squat about this mess and we can't wait no longer. The job's yours stranger, if you want it."

It was one way to get water, the drifter admitted to himself, but the situation still made him a bit uneasy. He wasn't going to agree to anything until he was satisfied that he had gotten the whole story.

"That's all fine and good," the cowboy stated, "but there must be a dozen other men in these parts that could take care of this for you. No reason it has to be me, is there?"

"You seen a dozen other men as look like they'll take the job?" Ezra sighed. "Sam was the one fella willing to go down there and when he didn't come back the rest of the folks said you'd have to be an idiot or mad to go in after him."

The cowboy nodded, "So you just waited until the first idiot or madman came riding into town and sent your little girl out to lure him in." It wasn't a question.

"Uh-yea," the chicken farmer agreed. "That's about the size of it."

The bluntness of the admission convinced the cowboy that he had all the facts, such as they were. If the drifter wasn't crazy for agreeing to go down in that well, he surely would be after another day without water. That was enough to decide the matter for him.

It only took a few minutes to clear the bricks away and lift the lid from the protective crate that kept anything else from getting in or out of the town's water supply. Once revealed, the well's opening yawned like the mouth of a giant snake, deep and forbidding. A long, frayed rope, tied around the base of the rock cylinder, twisted and drifted into the darkness bellow. Ezra lit a lantern, its greasy yellow glow a contrast to the orange of the late afternoon sun, and handed it to the stranger.

"You don't have to show me no carcass or nothing," the thin man explained, "Just fill up your canteen down there and show me that you're willing to drink from it when you get back and I'll be satisfied that you done your job."

"What should I look for?" the cowboy asked as he secured the lantern to his belt. He had read that sometimes the various stuffs of the earth seeped into water and made it unfit to drink, but he couldn't fathom what kind of beast could turn it foul. "Bunch of scorpions, maybe?"

"Don't know," Ezra replied as he stepped away from the stranger. "Might not be much for you to do at all, if it's just some animal died and's rotting in the water. Course, if that's all it is, it don't explain why Sam never came back up."

Sam. The name echoed through the cowboy's mind as he handed his hat to Ezra and hitched his legs over the rim of the well. He began the slow, unnerving descent into the inky blackness wondering, *Now what in the hell happened to Sam?*

It was a long, careful descent to the bottom of the well. Initially the walls of the vertical stone tunnel had been dry, but the closer he got to the bottom the more damp and treacherous the way became. His shoulders were filled with a fiery ache as his boots met the ground with a splash. The cowboy stood a moment to savor the sensation of the earth beneath him again, though the bottom of the well wasn't quite as he expected.

"This ain't right," he muttered to himself as he undid the lantern from his belt. There should have been a couple of feet of water here if the locals had been hauling it up with a bucket, yet the shallow pool in which the cowboy stood barely reached the bottom of his spurs. What was more distressing than that mystery, however, was the prospect of heading into the dark tunnel that lead off to his left. The opening gaped like a jagged mouth and, when he bent to look in, he was met with the overwhelming odor of decay. Whatever he'd come to find undoubtedly would be found through there, stench and all.

The stranger stood upright and stifled a gag as he pulled a red handkerchief from his back pocket and tied it around his face, just over the nose. He didn't have a lot of faith that it would help, but it offered a small amount of comfort. "No use putting it off," his lips murmured beneath their crimson covering as he dropped into a crouch and shimmied his way through the gap in the round stone wall.

The cowboy had crawled only a few feet when he felt the ceiling open up above him. Rising to one knee he held his lantern above his head and realized that he was in the middle of a shallow stream that ran along the edge of an underground cavern. In one of his father's books (perhaps the same one in which he had read about subterranean streams and mineral seepage) were stories about miles of natural caves that lay under the dessert, but he hadn't figured that he'd ever wind up in one himself.

It didn't take long to locate the source of the wretched aroma that had first assaulted the cowboy's nostrils. About fifteen feet away, just at the water's edge, lay a pile of pale ropey entrails enmeshed in tattered bits of skin and cotton britches and what might have been the broken-off handle of a pitchfork. Not far from that atrocity was a single black work boot with a jagged splinter of bone protruding from the top. "Holy Christ on His throne," the cowboy whispered into the rounded walls of the cavern. "What'n the hell could have done that?"

Instinctively, the stranger reached for his gun belt and loosed the six-shooter in its holster. He resisted the urge to draw it just yet, since keeping it dry was his first priority until he made his way out of the shallow stream. Carefully, he shuffled through the water, knowing full well that there could be an unseen drop beneath the surface, until he was well onto the rocky bank. Once there, he pulled the bandana from his mouth and gulped a lungful of the cool, damp air. He was still aware of the stench, but he was also aware that he'd been nearly holding his breath since he entered the murky cavern.

Skirting what was left of what had probably been Sam, the cowboy began walking along the edge of the water, searching for the point where the cavern ended and the water continued underground. His eyes darted about cautiously searching for whatever might be contaminating the water, such as the oil that Albert theorized or the dead animal that Ezra had guessed. His mind could not conceive of anything that could reduce a man to a waterlogged pile of guts, especially since the setting was unnerving enough without him trying to spook himself on top of it. For all he knew, Sam could have broken an ankle and been attacked by a coyote while he was down. Never mind how the hell a coyote would have gotten to the bottom of the well in the first place.

All around the cowboy, gaping tunnel mouths dotted the limestone walls, formed by eons of running water and who knew what all else. Some of them were as small as his fist and at least two were large enough to drive a wagon through, at least if the driver didn't sit too tall. Several times the stranger thought he saw motion in those hidden depths, but he knew that he could not trust his own senses amidst the dancing shadows and reflections that the lantern threw everywhere. About thirty yards from where he had left the edge of the shallow stream, the cowboy met the unmoving surface of the cavern wall. Just as he had predicted, the water continued to flow beneath the earth through a fissure far too low for him to traverse. "Guess I'll have to check the other end..." his musing was cut short by the sound of pebbles splashing in the water behind him.

The cowboy slid his palm fluidly around the pearl handle of his firearm. In a single, supple motion he turned, drew the weapon from its holster, cocked the hammer into place, and pointed it at the darkness behind him. There was nothing.

"Damn," he muttered, releasing a ragged breath and lowering his six-shooter to his side, easing the hammer down. Before he could take another step he saw the darkness in the space just above and in front of him suddenly begin to pour downward. The image was mystifying. He watched the shadow ooze to the floor and flow upright again into the vague shape of a man. The cowboy held his lantern before him, certain that it was a trick his agitated mind was playing. Then he saw the light reflect off the slick surface of glistening black skin.

The stranger stood frozen as a slimy, man-shaped thing began to unfold itself into sheets of ropey tentacles that had been hiding a giant tatter of a mouth where a torso should have been. The horror writhed and stretched itself until it was like a huge flag of abominable flesh waving in some evil breeze. Suddenly, the cowboy's paralysis broke and his gun was up and firing. The sound was like a cannon in the confines of the cavern, deafening the stranger and causing a low rumble to spread through the earth all around.

Like a bullwhip, a tentacle shot out and smashed down on the cowboy's wrist, sending the firearm pinwheeling through the air until it disappeared into the shallow stream. Reflexively the stranger jerked his hand back, ripping out threads of flesh where tiny barbs had hooked into it. The creature seemed to pulse as it moved forward in shambling pursuit, its mouth opening into a terrible spiral of needle-like teeth that surrounded a purple octopus of a tongue.

Another tentacle had slid unseen along the ground and wrapped itself around the cowboy's right ankle, jerking him upward until his shoulders crashed painfully into the unyielding limestone floor. In a motion fueled by pure terror and adrenaline, the stranger swung out with his left hand and brought the lantern crashing into the monster's face, just as it was lowering itself to consume him. Glass shattered and lamp oil poured out as liquid flame, engulfing the creature and causing it to stagger backward, lashing wildly at the air.

Whether the fire would be enough to stop the horror never occurred to the cowboy as he scrambled blindly back into the stream and towards entrance. He felt his six-shooter beneath his knee as he fled and unconsciously snatched it up in a death grip as he made his way to the bottom of the well. As soon as he was standing upright again, he felt calm enough to notice that a thick black smoke was pouring off of the burning creature and filling the cavern. Reflexively he squeezed his eyes shut and held his breath. If the monster's presence was enough to poison the water, surely the burning carcass would be toxic as well.

Tucking his gun into the waist of his trousers, the cowboy groped blindly until he found the rope and began climbing as fast as his fear-wracked body would carry him, finally drawing in a ragged breath just as he thought his lungs would explode in his chest. About three quarters of the way up, he heard a tremendous rumbling from below, a split second before the sound of a great cracking echoed from beneath him. The earth rocked with enough force that he was certain he would be knocked loose and sent tumbling back into the darkness, but his terror strengthened his grip like a vice. There was no doubt that the cavern had collapsed and, hopefully, the entrance to that inky hell sealed forever.

The fading orange glow of evening was like a mother's embrace to the cowboy as he scrambled over the edge of the well and looked into the horrified face of Ezra James. "What the hell happened down there?" the grizzled farmer asked in a wavering voice.

The cowboy, whose settling nerves had not yet had time to accept the notion of terrible ancient evils lurking in the bowels of the earth, could only wipe the sweat from his face with a trembling hand. "Well's caved in," he said flatly, "I think you'd better move on." Then he took his hat and turned his back on the hellish well and the rest of the accursed town. His thirst would have to wait.

Chapter One

His name was Scott, and he was really a cowboy. Despite his name, however, he was not an actual Scotsman. He was actually a mix of things. Mostly he was what a person might call a standard American mongrel.

Scott's grandfather, an Irishman, had developed a taste for Chinese women, which is where the cowboy inherited his dark hair and muddy brown eyes. Most folks just assumed he was part Mexican or Indian, but it generally wasn't considered polite to ask. The cowboy's mother was the one who, as gorgeous a creature as she had been, spent her life being called a half-breed. Though she had been raised in a laundry house in one of many small mining towns in what would eventually become the glorious state of California, it was a cattleman who eventually won the pretty girl's heart and took her away from all that.

Of course the term *cattleman* is used here only out of respect for the dead. He was more of a cowpoke-of-all-trades than a true man of the ranges, and sometimes he was hired to do more than just get the doggies along. It was that dangerous and uncertain work that eventually got him killed and left his lovely bride with a young son, a boatload of local prejudice, and not but her laundry skills to survive by.

Somehow a pretty face always finds a way out of trouble, however, and eventually Scott's mother got the right cow shit stain out of the right shirt and found herself married to an honest man. Together they moved to Montana and lived their honest life and, if hard work and clean living were equal to longevity, they would have lived past a hundred. Unfortunately, winters were cruel, diseases were frequently misunderstood and misdiagnosed, and life on a ranch was just plumb full of hazards.

By the age of seventeen, the young cowboy found himself alone in the world and without any means of support. It seemed that his step-father's family did not care to have some unwanted mongrel inheriting anything quite so valuable as a Montana cattle ranch, nor did they even want him to stay on as a hand, given how terribly painful it was for them to be reminded of the past. And so, with his fairly respectable ranching skills, a healthy young gelding with breeding as mixed and confused as his own, and his step-father's six-shooter (he didn't bother to ask for that one before slipping it into his bedroll on the morning he set off) the world became his oyster, though it seemed like it was pretty tightly shut at that particular moment.

The gun wasn't the only thing of his step-father's that the young cowboy took away from those vast and lonesome acres, he also took the man's name. His mother had always been fond of calling the young cowboy *Xiaohu*, in light of how strong and wild he had been as a baby, and everyone else had simply called him *boy*, but neither of those names would have carried him too far in the great big world of the American West, and so he took to introducing himself as Scott (a nickname for Henry Prescott) at least in situations where a handle was required. If someone inquired as to his family name, he'd just shrug and say that he didn't have any family to speak of and thus no need to represent them. At first it stung him a little bit to admit that, but eventually he learned to say so without so much as a twitch at the corner of his mouth. The cowboy was hardly the first man who didn't care to be linked to any particular past and so most folks just let it go at that.

Scott didn't have the advantages of a powerful body or an advanced education, but his medium build was strong and wiry and he had read enough books at the ranch to feel as wise as any other boy in his late teens was entitled to feel. The young cowboy might have spent enough years with just his mother to have become a bit more sensitive and introspective than most lads of his day, but his years of sweat and toil were enough to keep him from becoming what a person might call *soft*.

The next few years that followed his unceremonious eviction from home were hard ones. Work was always plentiful, but finding it on those endlessly stretching plains took effort and not every boss was necessarily kind nor honest. There had been more than one time when a rough shove back out the door and a few thinly veiled threats were all the reward he received in exchange for the sweat of his brow, but the cowboy chose to let those experiences thicken his skin, rather than break his spirit. That didn't mean it didn't hurt, however. There were times when he was riled until he was fit to be tied and didn't quit pounding on a pay house door until he heard the click-clack of a rifle being readied on the other side. Those were the days that truly changed him from his mother's little tiger into a lean and hungry wolf of the ranges.

But, tiger or wolf, he still had to guard that soft spot he had for other folks who were down on their luck. He was the kind of fella who would give his last nickel to buy oats for a trail hand's hungry horse, just because he couldn't stand the thought of another creature having a belly as empty as his own. Scott was young and skilled and could always earn another couple of bits. At least that was what he told himself when he handed over his last cigarette paper or bit of jerky to the guy sitting across from him at the campfire. To the people he called friends, for the short time he was with them, the cowboy was a right good man, to the people who hired him, however, he was just a loner with no one to watch his back if he was foolish enough to try to stand his ground.

It was in that spirit of giving, often considered peculiar to men of his stock and supposed character, that the cowboy found himself in a dusty little town with a poisoned well and, shortly thereafter, found himself a few miles away standing shakily next to his horse and wondering what the hell had just happened. He was beginning to wonder if he might not lose the next hand he held out to aid a stranger.

Chapter Two

Scott laid a calloused palm across the dappled neck of Windkicker and the horse nickered amiably. The animal was mostly grey and white, but patches of brown cropped up here and there at random. Windkicker wasn't likely to win any beauty contests, for certain, but he was strong and loyal and he didn't ask stupid questions. And, given that he was the cowboy's only company, he was generally the recipient of a lot of his two-legged companion's suppositions about life and the human condition. Although he may not have asked many questions, he certainly was on the receiving end of quite a few. Scott was a talkative fellow at times and he didn't let the fact that the sole member of his listening audience was wearing a saddle keep him from giving it a good earful when he had the mind to.

As the sky slowly turned its bruised twilight purple, the cowboy looked dead into the black pools of his horses eyes and asked, "You think I should go back?" Windkicker jerked his head slightly upwards in the response he gave to most of the questions that came his way, but it seemed pretty obvious to Scott that if he cared much for his personal wellbeing, then he should leave that shadow-haunted little dustbowl behind forever. Of course, that didn't necessarily mean that he would.

The cowboy had had good reason to run away from a great many things in his life, from charging bulls to whizzing bullets, but this was the first time that Scott felt truly ashamed to have done so.

After all, hadn't he made it back out of the well alive? And what about that widower and his daughter? It was all well and good for most drifters--those jaded individuals who perpetually had their eye on that next dusty street on the horizon--to turn a deaf ear and blind eye to their plight but that was simply not in Scott's nature. Even if he couldn't do much more than he had already done, he was going to go back. The way he saw it, Scott could return to the little settlement right at that moment, or he could travel a few more days until the guilt built up enough that he'd reared Windkicker around and waste a couple more sunrises making his way back. In the end, and with the implied consent of his trusty steed, he opted for the former.

Dark Rivers

The town of Drum Hollow had a population of about eighty people, if a person were to include whoever happened to be staying in the rooms above the saloon in their count. It consisted of a small grid of three streets running east and west and two cutting across them from north to south. The main street was boarded by about seven or eight businesses, each tucked snugly against its neighbor with a false front that gave it the appearance of greater stature than was actually warranted. There were a few stunted trees scattered here and there among the private dwellings, but for the most part there was little else but scraggly weeds sprouting up in the shady spots to break up the monotony of dry, grey earth and hot, white sunlight.

Drum Hollow, oasis though it might have been, was not a place a traveler felt inclined to stay unless no other options were available to him. There were other towns, just as small and equally remote, that somehow managed to have more of a life about them. The daylight hours were bustling with people going about their daily business and every sunset brought with it the raucous sounds of drifters and ranch hands blowing off steam in the saloons. Drum Hollow, however, had a quiet anemic quality about it. Whereas the legendary towns like Tombstone or Deadwood might be considered to be the overgrown bullies of the West, Drum Hollow was the pale kid in the corner that the other children whispered about but didn't dare approach for fear of catching something.

But if there was really anything of interest to be whispered about Drum Hollow, it would have been pretty hard to guess just what that might be. People from the surrounding countryside came to town to buy supplies, get a haircut, or settle a dispute with the sheriff (when he was kind enough to oblige the people with his presence) and little else. During slightly more prosperous times, there had been two saloons to while away the hours in, but eventually one had given up the ghost, which left Albert's as the only alternative. That suited the residents well enough, however, as they hardly had money for one shot of watered down whisky, let alone two. As its name suggested, Drum Hollow was merely a shell of a town and with each passing year it seemed to fade a little more back into the nothingness from which it had sprung.

When the cowboy rode back in from the east, he felt his guilt kick in a little harder. The sun-bleached buildings seemed to huddle together like rotting teeth beneath the newly fallen darkness, almost as if they were afraid the cowboy was going to kick them out of contempt. After all, what more could they could expect from an hombre heartless enough to leave a little girl and her father to die of thirst. Of course Scott was well aware of the absurdity of buildings feeling frightened, but that did not fade the impression in the least.

Besides having run off after his encounter in the subterranean cavern, the cowboy reflected, as he surveyed his surroundings from a new perspective, he had also managed to collapse said cavern in the process, though thankfully not enough to sink any nearby buildings. His initial instinct had assured him that it was all for the best, but since the fear-fueled fire had burned out of his blood, he realized that it simply meant that no one could go back and make things right. The water was poisoned at that point in its underground journey and now it would have to stay that way. That also meant that there was little and less that a wandering cowpoke could do just because he grew enough spine to come back and face up to the mess he had made.

The bottom line, however, was that it really was still his mess, even if he hadn't meant for it to be, and he was going to at least *ask* if there wasn't something that he could do to help set it right. At the very least, he could help the man and his daughter relocate to somewhere new or try to locate some water to get them by until they could figure out what they wanted to do. The cowboy doubted that Albert was going to be offering up any of his personal supply, whatever that mysterious source might be, from the kindness of his heart and the days weren't going to get much cooler anytime soon.

Scott took Windkicker's reins and looped them about the hitching post in front of the saloon for the second time that day. The only other animals present were a fly-bitten old mare and what appeared to an enormously fat burro. How any animal could grow so plump in such an environment was a mystery that the cowboy mentally filed away to ponder at another time. The sun was little more than a bloody smear just below the western horizon by that point and a billion stars shone merrily overhead, their cheery countenance oblivious to the trouble and misery that seemed to continuously play itself out beneath them.

At least the night air was cool, the cowboy reflected as he adjusted the battered rim of his hat, though that brought little comfort to his almost painfully parched throat. In all the commotion of the past few hours, he had been able to forget about the sandpaper that seemed to line his windpipe but, guilt or no, he was going to need to get something wet into his body and soon. Albert might not part with water, but surly the old codger must have had a bottle of something other than whisky tucked away beneath the bar. Hell, by that point Scott would have given his last nickel for a cold cup of that morning's leftover coffee, if such a drink even existed in Drum Hollow.

The batwing doors swung easily aside and the cowboy found that the establishment had not changed much since his last visit. The same two grizzled old coots were playing cards in the corner, only now another slightly younger man leaned against the wall and watched their game with eyes dulled by boredom and cheap liquor. A middle-aged man wearing a grey suit and matching handlebar mustache sat at a table by a silent and dusty piano. Judging by the cleanliness of his clothes and the bowler hat sitting on the table next to his newspaper, Scott guessed that he was a local business man. Although apparently more affluent than his other whisky-sipping colleagues, his expression was no more lively nor alert. When his gaze and the cowboy's met, he simply nodded uncomfortably and decided that his paper was suddenly infinitely more fascinating than it had been the moment before.

Albert himself was leaning across the bar on his elbows, picking at his teeth with a splinter of wood. He had noted the cowboy's approach before the other men in the bar, but appeared to be no more enthused than they. Still, he pushed himself upright and addressed the returning customer. "You change your mind about that whisky, sir?" he asked. The yellow-toothed smile that split his face in the asking was more ghastly than reassuring, but Scott thought that it was preferable to the almost mindless visages of the other men in the saloon.

The cowboy's worn boots thudded heavily against the grimy wood floor as he approached the bar. He noted, with some surprise, the lack of stools that he would have expected to be lining the front. In most of the bars and road houses he'd made his way to, there were seats in front of the bar during the quieter hours which were quickly pushed against the walls once the crowd got livelier and space was at a premium. He was finding it harder and harder to imagine that Albert's was ever a particularly raucous establishment and guessed that whatever stools there might have once been had long since been broken down for firewood. It was a small detail, but it added to already unwelcoming feel of the place.

"Well," Scott asked, that first word coming out hoarse and cracked, "What have you got that's wet?"

The unnatural smile dropped away from Albert's face like a clock falling off a wall. "I thought I told you before, stranger." Scott did not fail to notice that he had already been demoted from *sir* back to *stranger*.

"You said there was no water for sale," the cowboy replied. "But surely you've got something else stashed back there behind the bar. Maybe a keg or two?"

Albert's mustache twitched in irritation. He was not used to being pressed by anyone, let alone a peach-fuzzed whelp who talked like his nickel was the last one on earth. Still, he couldn't very well afford to turn away business if business was to be had. "I might," he finally admitted, "but it'll cost you more than some lousy five cents. You hear?"

Scott nodded. "I hear you. What've you got?"

With an exaggerated huff of effort, Albert dropped behind the bar and came up with a bottle that would have looked at home in the cellar of a haunted old castle. The glass had probably been clear at one time, but now it was so caked with grime that it was impossible to even see what was inside. The paper label remained faithfully pasted in place but time and water spots had obliterated whatever had once been printed there. It could have been a bottle of sand for all anyone could tell.

The barkeep rubbed a thumb against the surface of the glass but it did nothing the reveal the contents of the bottle and resulted in little more than blackening his flesh. "Well?" he asked impatiently as the cowboy stared dumbly down at it.

"Well what?" Scott replied.

"Do you want some or not?" Albert was clearly losing what little there was left of his patience. "It's two bucks a glass."

Scott snorted a laugh, "You're shitting me. Unless that's a bottle of Christ's own tears, I'm not giving you two day's pay even if you offered me the whole damn thing."

Albert set the bottle heavily onto the bar. "Look," he explained, the tone of his voice carefully controlled. "You asked what I got that ain't whisky and this is it. I don't get beer no more since it don't keep long and the boys don't seem to care for it anyway. Now my pappy bought this here wine in Chicago, you ever heard of it?" The cowboy nodded patiently and the barkeep continued,

"Well that's a helluva long way from here and a helluva long time ago so this shit is worth a lot more to me than you're likely to ever be. So you want some or not?"

The cowboy let out a long dry sigh and considered his situation. He wasn't in a position to bargain, but he also wasn't in a position to fork over two bucks for a glass of anything that didn't come served in the Holy Grail itself. "Look," he finally asked, "You got anything to eat in here?"

"Now you want food, do ya?" Albert said crossing his arms in front of his chest. "Well I've got a couple of biscuits left from breakfast and I could probably see to getting you a chunk of jerky, but that's all. The supply wagon's behind this week and I can't be giving nothing away that I might need myself."

Scott nodded. "Okay, I tell you what. You give me those biscuits and jerky and, say," he paused to give the appearance of thoughtfully considering the bargain, "a half glass of what's in the bottle and I'll give you a dollar."

"What the hell kind of deal is that?" Albert demanded.

The cowboy gestured around the room, "As good as you're likely to get tonight, my friend." The corner of Albert's mustache twitched at being called *friend*. "Besides, you and I both know that there ain't a thing in this whole saloon, short of that piano over there, worth more than a buck, and if you try to squeeze any more blood from this stone I'm just gonna take my money and walk out and you can see how rich those biscuits make you without me."

"Damnation," Albert scowled and brought up a filmy glass tumbler and set it on top of the bar. The older man's jowls fairly quivered with irritation as he began to peel away at the wax atop the bottle with a blackened thumbnail. "You just be grateful that I'm a generous man," Albert instructed his customer. "I don't owe you nothing but the back of my hand for coming into my place and trying to order me around like that, you bellowing young calf. But I'll take your money easy enough and you'll get something in your belly. After that, though, I want you gone. There ain't no place in this bar for you nor none of your kind in this town. You understand me?"

The cowboy was very close to asking if that meant that getting a room for the night was out of the question, but he felt that he'd pushed his luck far enough. Albert might have been more bluster than bite, but he was proud of his position in the town, such as it was, and it was only natural that he didn't take kindly to anything that even remotely sounded like a challenge to his authority. Scott felt that he, himself, had been as polite and reasonable as was warranted, but he had learned on more than one occasion that his particular perspective on a given situation was not always shared, let alone appreciated.

"Now let me see your silver, cowpoke," Albert demanded. The bottle was not yet open and it didn't seem like it was going to be until there was some cash out in the open.

"Let's see them biscuits," Scott replied.

"Fair enough," the barkeep admitted, but the tone of his voice suggested that he thought it was anything but fair. He went around to a back room and came back with a battered pewter plate adorned with three slightly burnt baking powder biscuits and a chunk of jerky roughly the size of half a shriveled peach. It was as pathetic a meal as the cowboy had ever been duped into paying for, but at least it was food.

"Now then," Albert repeated as if talking to a difficult child, but his unfriendly tone mellowed somewhat when he saw the heavy silver coin the cowboy pulled out of the leather pouch laced into his belt. The only thing Albert loved more than his pride was his money and it didn't take much convincing to get him to trade one for the other. The barkeep snatched the coin away almost faster than it was offered, as if he worried that it might up and fly away if he didn't pounce the very moment it was slapped onto the scuffed wood of the bar.

The contents of the bottle, it turned out, was a very eye-watering vintage of 1823 white vinegar. Although the grimy glass cylinder had once contained a sweet dry wine that had, in fact, come all the way from Italy before being sold to Albert's father in Chicago, it had not been properly preserved amidst all of its pre-Drum Hollow travels. It appeared that Albert knew a great deal more about hawking liquor than storing it and the result, at least in that case, was completely undrinkable.

Rather than part with a single cent of his hard earned dollar, Albert eventually relented and provided the cowboy with a battered tin cup of warm but nonetheless *ambrosial* water. The barkeep was extremely secretive about where he had drawn the liquid from, some mysterious source near wherever the biscuits had come from no doubt, but assured the cowboy that it was safe to drink and even took a small sip himself to prove it.

It was the most expensive cup of water that the young cowboy had ever had in his life, but it was also the sweetest. He carefully sipped at it while choking down the dry salty contents of his dinner, savoring each drop as if it were really worth what he had paid. For those few precious seconds it spent sliding down his parched throat, he almost believed that it was.

When the meal was over, only a matter of a few minutes, really, Scott straightened himself up and brushed a few crumbs from the red bandana that still hung loosely around his neck. The cowboy hadn't bothered to take a seat at any of the empty tables, preferring to stand and finish his business almost as quickly as his reluctant host wanted him to. With a final longing glance into the dented bottom of his cup he stated, "I guess I'll be on my way then."

"I guess you will," Albert agreed, scooping the plate and cup away with an impatient gesture that suggested that the cowboy had somehow been an inconvenience to the other paying customers.

Scott headed towards the door and stopped halfway before turning and asking, "You know where a man named Ezra lives?"

"Ezra James?" the barkeep inquired.

"That'd be the one," the cowboy assured him. "I need to speak with him about some business from earlier today."

"And what kind of business might that be?"

"None that you'd want to trouble yourself about," Scott said in an even voice.

"You got that right, boy," Albert said leaning once again in his familiar slouch over the bar. "There's been trouble enough around here for one day. Between you and the quake we just had, I know I've had my fill. Now why don't you just get along then and stop pestering me with your pointless questions?"

"He lives a small place in the southeast corner of town," a timid voice called out from near the piano. "He's the only one in these parts with chickens, so you can't miss it."

Scott turned towards the speaker. It was the man with the newspaper, who had an expression of some little pride on his face. Apparently, he was pleased to have some information of value to offer the stranger.

"Much obliged," the cowboy thanked him with a tip of his hat and watched as the smile melted away from the businessman's face. Scott was unable to see the withering glare that Albert was shooting in that direction, but he could feel it enough for the small hairs on his neck to prickle. Knowing that his welcome had been worn out well before he had even slipped out of his saddle, he gave the gray-suited man a final nod of appreciation and stepped back into the night.

Chapter Three

Windkicker was waiting dutifully where he had been left shortly before, but the overly affectionate nuzzle he offered his rider upon the cowboy's return suggested that the horse had enjoyed his animal company no more than the cowboy had enjoyed his. It appeared that Drum Hollow did not discriminate by species when it came to making visitors feel unwelcome. "Don't you worry, boy," the cowboy assured his mount. "We won't linger in these parts any longer than we have to."

As sweet as the water had been passing through Scott's lips, he knew it would be no less so for his horse. Windkicker was a patient beast, but that outward calm didn't mean there wasn't a painful thirst hiding underneath. If Ezra had a daughter and chickens, then he'd have at least a little of the wet stuff, even if it was just an old rain barrel. Considering how the cowboy had risked his life earlier to help the poor man out, a few gulps for his horse wasn't an unreasonable request.

Besides, the cowboy somehow felt in his gut that his business with old Ezra was far from complete.

As dark as it was by that point, Scott and his horse had no trouble finding the James' property. Although the rider could not see the chickens sleeping snugly inside of their coop, he had no trouble smelling them. The dry dusty scent of droppings hung like an invisible cloud that felt as if it settled right into a man's skin on contact. It was a familiar odor that the cowboy had never much cared for.

A soft orange glow emanated from a single window of a fairly pathetic little shack. The extremely modest building could be called a home only if the speaker was feeling particularly poetic in his description of it. The house on the Prescott ranch where the cowboy had spent his formative years had been a real home with a porch, stone fireplace, and a comforting sense of welcome about it. The building where Ezra James and his daughter retired for the night would have been better suited to store tack or feed than to shelter and comfort human beings.

The cowboy was pleased, however, to see that there was indeed a rain barrel nestled against the west side of the building where the slope of the tin roof managed to direct the precious drops of liquid when they were kind enough to make an appearance. Scott quietly dismounted and started leading his horse directly to what he hoped would be a reasonable quantity of rain water. Windkicker's hooves made only a soft *whoomp* sound on the dusty earth outside the shack, but it was evidently enough to alert the patriarch of the little residence.

"Who's out there?" The voiced carried so well through the thin walls and into the still evening air that both the cowboy and his mount were started by its clarity and halted in place. When the visitor didn't answer quickly enough Ezra continued with a warning. "I've got a rifle pointed out at you, stranger. And my trigger finger ain't feeling none too patient tonight."

"Now just hold on there, hoss." The cowboy found his voice. Although Scott was fairly certain that the combination of lamplight and the grimy glass of the window would prevent anyone in the house from seeing clearly enough to make a clean shot, he wasn't in the mood to dodge any wild ones, either. "Hold on," he continued. "It's me, from before. I'm the guy you sent down the well. Remember?"

There was a pause and the cowboy could see the shape of the man inside cupping his hands and pressing his face against the window. Again Scott doubted that anyone in the house could see more than a vague shadow, but Ezra seemed satisfied. "Okay. I see ya. What'er you doing back here? I thought you and that yellow stripe on your back would be half way to Baltimore by now, fast as you hightailed it out of here afore."

The cowboy bristled at the insinuation of cowardice, but he had to admit that he *had* left in an awful hurry that afternoon. "I regret that I gone off like I did." Scott didn't like apologizing for running away from a horrible ungodly monster under the earth, something any reasonable man would do, but he apologized just the same. "But seeing as how it ain't right to leave a widower and his child in such dire straits, I come back to see if I can't do something to make up for it."

Windkicker, not feeling particularly moved by his companion's apology, had already taken advantage of the distraction (along with the slack in his reins) and moved close enough to the rain barrel to drop his head deep inside. The echo of the horse's slurps inside the barrel suggested that any moisture inside was pretty far down.

"Now you get that beast outta my water!" Ezra protested and suddenly the door to the shack was thrown open and the grizzled chicken farmer stepped out in the same overalls he'd been wearing earlier in the day, an ancient muzzle-loader clenched in his gnarled fists. His expression was a mix of anger at the theft of his water combined with the terror of what it would mean if his tiny supply of moisture was used up without warning.

The cowboy immediately pulled back on the reins and eased his mount away from the old barrel, sorry that he could not offer his horse more, but sorrier still that such a little drink meant such hardship to the poor man standing in the doorway. "I apologize for Windkicker's bad manners," Scott began, "but let's say that little drink of his calls us even for our earlier trouble. I won't ask for no more."

Ezra's grip on the old firearm loosened and he nodded. "Ayuh. Even it is then." Angry as he was the moment before, it sounded like the poor farmer was glad that his debt was settled so easily. There was many a wandering cowpoke who would have taken a great deal more than a drink for their horse had they come sneaking by in the dark of night. No doubt reflecting upon just such a thought, Ezra looked back into the shack to reassure himself that his daughter was still safe and untouched.

The cowboy understood his power in the situation and tried not to make an issue of it. Scott was young, armed, and had come to a man's home unannounced in the night with a debt to settle. Ezra, on the other hand, was a broken man with nothing to protect his daughter with, other than a solid work ethic and an old riffle he didn't even have the ball and powder to load. Had the cowboy been one of the disreputable men whom he'd had the misfortune of working with from time to time, things could have gone much worse for the widower and his daughter.

"Look, Mr. James," the cowboy began keeping both of his hands on the reins of his horse and away from his holster, "I didn't come here to cause any trouble, though I did dearly need a drink for my horse. I'm sorry that it meant so much to you, but I'd like to see if I can't make it up to you some."

"I said we're even, so you don't owe me nothing," the widower said, his arm dropping protectively across the shoulder the curious little girl who had finally come to the door to see what all the hoopla was about. "If'n you just ride right back on out of town, we can forget the whole thing. You don't need to worry none about me telling folks you're yellow. I don't know what you saw down in that well, so I ain't in no place to say you weren't right to run from it."

Scott let out a deep sigh. It was clear that that Ezra James would be more comfortable *not* having the cowboy around, even if he was offering to help. Still, the lone wolf cowpoke felt a sense of duty and took pride that he put that before his own comfort. He might not have had a lot to call his own in the world, but his mother had raised him to be a good man and that was something that he lost only when he walked away from situations like he found himself in at that moment.

"I thank you for your understanding, sir," the cowboy acknowledged, "but it ain't right for me to ride off and leave you two in the kind of trouble I know you're in. The way I see it, I can either help you find a new source of water or help you move out of Drum Hollow to some better place. Whichever of those suits you best, I mean to see to in whatever way I can."

The widower looked down at Lizzy's face for a moment and saw her expectant eyes staring back up at his. "Alright then, cowboy. Why don't you see to your horse and come in for a spell? I guess it ain't so late that a man can't show a few manners to a guest."

It took only a moment for Scott to secure Windkicker to a hitching post that was no doubt left over from a time when the old widower had had a mount of his own. At the moment, it was little more than a sad reminder of just how hard times had become.

The interior of the little shack was filled with many more such reminders. There was a rough-hewn table with three chairs, a cast-iron stove, and a couple of straw pallets with a thin and fading quilt draped over the two of them. The only other contents of note were a few tin dishes, a pitted washtub, and a cracked leather book that was no doubt the family bible.

"There used to be more," Ezra explained as he hung his rifle on two metal brackets above the door, "but I had to sell it bit by bit over the years. My wife, God rest her gentle soul, put up with a lot staying with me." The chicken farmer's eyes misted over as he remembered his lost lover, only a few days in the ground. It seemed like he was going to say more but then cleared his through and regained his composure. "I don't plan on leaving here anytime soon, given as I don't have no place else to go to. So what do you think you can do about the water problem? You any good at digging wells?"

The cowboy actually did have some experience digging wells, but it was not a task he would have wanted to take on without more help than a grieving farmer and his child daughter could muster. What was worse, ironically, was that digging a well was very thirsty work and he doubted he would even survive the attempt dig down deep enough before the summer sun did him in for good. "Why hasn't anybody else tried to dig a new well yet?" Scott inquired.

Ezra scratched at the silvery stubble under his chin. "I reckon somebody'll try pretty quick here. Now that the old well has collapsed in that little quake you caused, there's not much choice. I don't know how much luck they'll have, though."

"What about creeks? You know of any off the beaten path?" Scott was pretty sure he knew the answer to that question before he asked it, but it was better to make sure. People could be protective about information like that and just because he didn't know of one didn't mean one didn't exist.

The old chicken farmer shook his head. "You think that skinflint Albert wouldn't take your money for water if'n he knew there was more nearby?" When the cowboy seemed surprised that Ezra knew about that exchange he quickly explained. "Lizzy told me about you and Albert's little chat at the bar today and it don't surprise me in the least. Trust me, there's no secret stream the locals don't want strangers to know about. Leastwise, none that I'm privy to."

The prospect of helping the pathetic duo find a new home was sounding like the only option, whether or not Ezra wanted to admit it, but then the cowboy had one final idea. "When I was down in the well today, I noticed that the water came from a stream and there was a lot of tunnels and caves that branched off from there. Now, I'm guessing that if a new well is dug upstream from the cave-in, the water should still be clean."

"What was it making the water bad?" Lizzy spoke up for the first time since the cowboy's arrival. "Did you find a dead animal? Sam said that's all it was."

Scott shifted uncomfortably in his seat, "We can talk about that later."

Ezra nodded, "Yeah, I reckon that's just what will be done--digging a new well, I mean--but it's going to take time to do that."

"Exactly," the cowboy replied. "It's going to take time *and* water, too. Nobody can finish a job like that without food and water in the meantime. The way I see it, we need to find some source of water before that, even if we have to haul it in by wagon. If we find that, it'll buy enough time for the well to be finished and for things to get more or less back to normal in town."

"Ayuh," the widower agreed. "But I just said we ain't got no hidden stream or nothing. Where do suppose we're gonna find this other water we need?"

"That's what I mean about the caverns and caves," the cowpoke continued to explain. "I figure that there must be some way down into those caves from the surface level. If we find one of those, we might be able to make our way back down to the underground stream and haul water up from there. It's worth a shot, anyway."

"Worth a shot," Lizzy eagerly agreed, looking to her pa to make sure he, too, was willing to go along with the idea. Just why she seemed so keen on the cowboy's plan was anyone's guess, but a fellow would be hard pressed to find a child who didn't like the idea of hunting down a hidden cave.

"And," Scott added, "I noticed that the level of the stream was mighty low when I was down there. If we go looking, we might even find out if something isn't blocking up the source of the water, another cave-in maybe, and take care of that. When all is said and done, Drum Hollow might even end up with *more* water than it had before."

The cowboy was actually starting to feel a little excited by the prospect of venturing out to find hidden caves and secret sources of water. It was like something out of one of the yarns he'd sometimes hear around the campfire if the mood was right and a good storyteller was at hand.

After a moment of quiet, the old widower spoke up, "And what's in it for you? I ain't got nothing to give you for your trouble and ain't nobody in town like to pony up payment for help they didn't ask for. You seem like a good man, a little green maybe, but you gotta expect to get something out of this."

"I do," the cowboy admitted. "I expect that you'll give me a spot on your floor to sleep tonight and I expect a chicken dinner once we find enough water to take care of the town. How'd that do ya? I'm not a stranger to hunkering down in one place for a spell and then moving on. You don't got no cause to worry that I'll overstay my welcome."

"Is he really gonna stay here, Pa?" Lizzy asked. "We ain't got no more beds."

Scott lifted his hands up, "I got my own bedroll for that, little lady. I'm just asking for a place to lay it that's above the snakes and out of the wind."

Ezra shook his head. "I just don't get you, stranger. Just you coming back to this dried up cow flop of a town means you're gonna be hungry and thirsty longer than you need to be. Why'n the hell you'd want to stay more than you have to? This is real life, sir, not some penny dreadful where the hero rides in and saves us all from the man in the black hat. Ain't no quick duel at high-noon gonna take care of an empty belly. You get me?"

The cowboy did have to admit that he felt a little foolish for the starry-eyed way he'd just assumed he'd be able to make things better, but that didn't mean he wouldn't give it a try. "You got a bucket?" he asked.

"Yes sir," Ezra admitted. "I do."

"All I'm asking is to borrow that and a little of your time. If my scheme turns out to be nothing but day dreams and hogwash, I'll be out of your hair and you'll be no worse for the trouble."

And with that, it was settled.

Chapter Four

As the cowboy sat at the table, the morning light casting a ruddy orange glow across the freshly oiled pieces of his six-shooter, he considered his plan for the day. Ezra and Lizzy were out tending to the chickens and, the cowboy suspected, paying their respects at the humble but well-tended grave behind the little shack. That bit of business gave Scott a moment to reflect upon what might be the best plan of action for the day.

It was going to be a long hot spell out exploring the expanse near the town--poking behind bushes and under boulders for the entrance to a cave that might or might not be there. The three of them would be able to take along a little of the rainwater in the cowboy's canteen and a few withered apples, but nothing that would qualify as a proper meal. It was going to be a punishing experience, Scott knew that at the outset, but Ezra had agreed to let him try out his plan and that's just what he meant to do.

"We might as well set off early," Ezra said as he made his way through the splintery wooden slats that served as a front door. "It's only gonna get hotter from here on out."

The cowboy had already reassembled his firearm and had been spinning the chamber absently while he waited for the morning chores to be finished. He started filling it with bullets when his host came back in, though Scott could only hope that they were still fit to fire. Given that the cowboy had only a handful of extra rounds tucked into the slots of his gun belt, there weren't many to spare. "Yeah. I reckon it's now or never, eh?"

"Whatcha need that for?" Lizzy asked from over the back of a chair as the cowboy holstered his weapon. "You fast enough to shoot a snake?"

The young cowboy grinned. "I don't believe I've ever tried that, little lady, but it might be we see something tastier than a rattler out there and I mean to be ready to take it down and fill our bellies with it."

Satisfied with the response, the little girl retreated to grab a sun bonnet from the corner of the room. It was clearly too big for her and slipped down almost to her nose. "Why don't you wear your own, pumpkin?" Ezra asked.

"I wanna wear Mama's today. Is that okay?"

The chicken farmer's expression didn't change, but there was a slight crack in his voice when he gave his consent.

Without another word, Ezra stepped out into the sun with the cowboy and his daughter in tow. It was still early enough that the three-quarter moon was visible in the western sky but not even a wisp of a cloud could be seen in any direction. Had any of the three of them harbored any hopes for rain, they would have been dashed into the dusty earth right then.

Scott gave Windkicker a friendly pat on the nose and he untethered the beast and slung the bucket (a surprisingly new and sturdy one with a lantern and stubby little pickaxe tucked inside) over the horn of his saddle. When he asked Lizzy if she wanted to add their provisions to the horse's load she shook her head solemnly. Carrying their lunch was her only duty on the trip and she meant to take it seriously.

"Which way do you reckon we should head off?" Ezra asked as the explorers reached the edge of the dusty street.

"I was kind of hoping you had an idea," the cowboy admitted. "Being that you know the area better'n me and all."

The farmer shook his head. "I told you I don't know nothing about no hidden streams and such and I know even less about caves."

The two men stood there quietly for a moment and pondered the situation individually, preferring not to speak unless there was something worth drying a fellow's mouth over. Once the silence reached the point of being almost painful, the cowboy felt a tug at the side of his trousers. Looking down he had a sense of deja vu from the previous day as Lizzy looked up at him with the same solemn eyes. "You got an idea?" he asked.

"I know the place where the Jennings boys made their fort. That's kind of a cave." The little girl scrunched up her face as she thought on it further. "Ain't got no water in it though."

Ezra brow furrowed with displeasure at the admission. "What did I tell you about those Jennings boys, girl? I ought to tan your hide for running out to play in the dust with those little heathens. God forbid that—"

The cowboy held up a hand to cut the lecture off before it took itself too far. "Now you should always listen to your pa, Lizzie, and I suspect he's gonna have more to say to you on this subject later. But for now why don't you tell me where these boys like to play. It's as good a place to start as any, I suppose."

Ezra gave the little girl's arm a good pinch and she yelped like kicked dog. By the way she stuck her tongue out in response to the offense, however, it was clear that neither parent nor child was as upset as Scott had worried they might be. Rubbing her shoulder in mock distress, Lizzy pointed towards the east and explained, "It's over there."

"How far out do you figure?" the cowboy asked.

"I dunno. Maybe a couple of miles."

This time Ezra seemed a little more genuinely unhappy with the girl's admission. It was one thing for his eight year-old daughter to be hanging around with some rough-and-tumble lads from town, but it was something else entirely for her to be wandering miles away from home with them without Ezra having the least inkling of it.

"And when did you have time for that?" the farmer asked. "If your ma was here I'd warm your backside good and send you back to the house."

"Aw," Lizzy protested. "Ma knew about it. She said it was okay so long as the boys looked after me. It was our adventure!"

Ezra continued to frown as his daughter's confession continued, but he was in no place to argue with the decision made by his departed wife. "Well," he began, "just you don't be doing that no more, you hear? I got to have you where I can find you."

Lizzy's eyes started to mist over and two fat tears slid down her grimy pink cheeks as her father rested a protective hand on her head. "I won't do nothing foolish, Pa. I promised Momma that I'd look after you and I will."

The cowboy shifted uncomfortably as he witnessed the family exchange. "What say we get moving?" The father and daughter seemed a little relieved at the opportunity to turn their attention elsewhere. Without another word, the little group headed east into the morning sun.

It took a solid hour to reach the boulder strewn patch of scrub grass the Jennings boys had dubbed *Fort Blood-n-Guts*. There wasn't much to see and only a couple of kids, bored past their own ability to stay out of trouble, would have spent the time and energy to uncover the crevice that constituted the "cave" Lizzy had spoken of. No doubt countless riders had passed that spot, only a few dozen yards from the road itself, on their way in and out of town without guessing there was so much as a spot to piss in amidst the bristly flora.

The randomly scattered stones were a bit of an oddity, the cowboy reflected, given that there was no sign of a crumbled structure (natural or otherwise) or of any hill that they might have rolled down. Perhaps it had been the site of Indian rituals or some such thing, though he could hardly imagine what that might have been. The dog and cat-sized stones themselves were a rusty color and rough looking, as if the desert winds hadn't had time to smooth them out yet. If the out-of-place rocks held any secrets beyond the mystery of their own presence, however, they were doing a good job of keeping them to themselves. Scott lifted his hat a moment to run a hand through sweat slicked black hair and then pointed to the crevice. "You ever go in there, Lizzy?"

The little girl shook her head. "Lands, no! The boy's wouldn't let me into the heart of ole Blood-n-Guts. They said that was for soldiers only and that the womenfolk needed to stay outside and tend to gathering food and such."

The cowboy smirked, "That sounds like the kind of nonsense little boys tend to think of. And just what did they expect you to do out here if you was beset upon by outlaws?"

Lizzy's face became comically grim as she pondered what had been intended as a rhetorical question. "I guess I just would have had to protect them boys. A woman's got a lot of duties sometimes."

Ezra ignored his daughter's musings. "So do you reckon there was room in there for the three of you?" The red of his naked face and shoulders seemed to almost glow under the harsh yellow light of mid-morning, his battered straw hat offering scant protection. "Does it go back very far?"

"I think so," the little girl admitted. "They went in far enough as I couldn't see them no more."

The cowboy shifted his gunbelt and nodded. "This might be what we're looking for then, though we're gonna need to make that hole a little wider to get a grown man inside."

"Easy as that?" Ezra asked. "An hour out and we found what we need?"

"Might be," the cowboy admitted, "Though let's not start counting our buckets before they're wet."

"I ain't never heard it said like *that* before," Lizzy said.

"And I ain't never gone looking for water in a desert cave, but my own ma always said there's a first time for everything," Scott replied.

Windkicker, who was busy perusing the scrub grass for anything worth chewing on, didn't seem to mind when the bucket was lifted off of his back. "You just rest easy there, boy," Scott soothed the horse. "And don't go running off while we's working. You hear?"

"Not gonna tether him?" Ezra asked.

"Naw. He's smart enough to know one of these spindly bushes ain't strong enough to hold him if he don't want to be held. Besides, he's not like to go wandering too far." The cowboy gave Lizzy a little wink. "He gets lonely."

Chapter Five

It was thirsty work clearing away the stubborn weeds that lined the entrance to the crevice, and even more hacking away at the brittle stone with the pickaxe. Lizzy was content to sit to the side with the canteen in her lap, carrying it over to the two sweating men when a drink was called for. There wasn't a one of them who didn't want to gulp that whole thing down, but even Lizzy knew that a few sips at a time where all that could be spared.

It was maybe ninety minutes later when the cowboy called a halt and stood up to stretch the soreness out of his back. "I think I could get in there now," he surmised. "It'd still be a little tight, but we've cleared away as much dirt as we can and I don't think I've got it in me to start hacking away at solid rock."

Ezra pulled a filthy handkerchief from his back pocket and mopped the sweat from his face. "I won't argue with you there, son. I just wish we could see farther in. From here it looks like the hole don't go back no more than a couple of feet."

The cowboy nodded his agreement. "If what Lizzy says is true, them two boys went back in a ways. Maybe it don't go no farther than the span of a wagon or so, but I'm hoping it does. Could be that the kids stayed close to the opening just because they didn't have no light with them."

"They did say it was dark in there," Lizzy piped up. "And real cold, too."

"That's a good sign then," the cowboy admitted. "If there's cold air coming up, then it must be from deeper down than just a couple of feet. We'd probably have felt it ourselves, when we was digging, if the dadblasted sun wasn't beating down on us as it is."

After a few more minutes of quiet rest and reflection, the cowboy grabbed the bucket and tested it against the opening of the crevice. At first it wouldn't go down smoothly, but it was easy enough to warp it a little around the lip to make it fit. With that taken care of, Scott sat himself down and dangled his boots into the opening. "You wanna grab me the latern, Liz?"

The little girl, happy to be useful again, fetched it for him and handed it over with a satisfied grin. Ezra had already fished the box of matches out of his pocket and leaned down to light the wick, making sure the flame was turned down low.

"This is the only lantern I got," he reluctantly admitted, "seeing as how my other one didn't make it home yesterday. All the oil that's inside is all the oil I got, so go easy on it if you can."

The cowboy nodded his understanding. "I don't plan on being in there too long and, if that ends up being the case, I hope to bring something back up that makes it worth the expense."

Ezra and his daughter crouched down at the lip of the crevice as the cowboy slid the rest of the way in. When the brim of his hat caught on the edge, Lizzy reached out to push it down after him. "Be careful in there," Ezra warned, but the cowboy had no intention of being anything but.

If the Jennings boys had been right about anything in their lives, it was that it was indeed cold down in that hole. The cowboy surmised that the temperature must have been a solid twenty degrees lower just a few yards away from the opening. The cool atmosphere was damp and hung over him like a wet blanket, almost guaranteeing that a source of water was nearby. That was good news, but finding it without breaking his neck in the process was an entirely different matter.

Dark Rivers

The ground sloped at a sharp angle and was covered with treacherous little pebbles that threatened to unbalance the cowboy and his smooth-soled boots. Slowly and cautiously, he made his way deeper into the earth, at one point squeezing through a crevice so tight he was afraid he was going to have to leave the bucket behind.

How deep did them boys come down? the cowboy wondered. The dim light of the lantern revealed little more than pitted rock and shifting shadows, but it was a damn sight better than wandering around blindly. There was no telling when an unseen jut of rock might catch him in the eye or the floor might just drop away. Yes, sir. A man would have to be half mad to go in there without a light. *Hell,* he thought, *I'm half mad for coming in here* with *one.*

Although he had tried not to think about the encounter the day before, Scott couldn't completely drive away the image of that writhing black horror. Although he felt fairly certain that the world held no more secrets as unimaginably ghastly as that, the cowboy's gun sat loosely in its holster and his hand unconsciously caressed the pearl handle as he made his slow and steady progress. He nearly jumped out of his skin when he heard the echoing voice of Ezra calling down to him. The farmer's voice sounded so far away that it could have been coming from the dark side of the moon.

"You okay in there?" Ezra asked.

"Okay!" Scott shouted back, frowning at the way the cave walls seemed to diminish his words to a dull rumble. "Five more minutes!" He waited a few seconds for a reply and then continued to make his way deeper.

After another minute of deliberate shuffle-stepping, a minute that felt like it had to have been at least thirty, the cowboy heard the first sound in the tomb-like silence that hadn't originated from either himself or Ezra. It took him a second to recognize it for what it was but, when he did, it was all he could do to keep himself from charging forward.

It was the sound of running water.

The darkness continued to swallow up the lantern's faint glow so that it didn't reflect off the water until Scott had crouched down and shimmied to the very edge of the flow. If the cowboy hadn't heard it first, he might well have stepped right into the newfound treasure and been swept away by the underground torrent. The water was moving so quickly, in fact, that it nearly jerked the bucket out of his hand when he dipped it in to take a sample. As the cowboy fought against the gripping current, his arm was soaked up to the elbow by water cold enough to numb the skin almost on contact.

It's like a mountain stream in March, the cowboy reflected as he brought the rim of the well-chilled bucket to his nose and gave it a sniff. Other than the familiar tang of tin, the liquid didn't give off any of the punk smell he had been half afraid to check for. The lantern light shone strait to the bottom of the bucket as well, promising a cool drink as clear as it was odorless.

Dipping his hand in, Scott brought out some of the icy liquid and tested it first with his tongue, followed by a cautious sip. After repeating that a few times, he felt satisfied enough to lower his face to the surface of the bucket and take in a deep satisfying slurp. Had it never occurred to the lone explorer that his body could sing with pure unadulterated pleasure, it occurred to him at that moment, and if there had been poison in that water, Scott could not have thought of a sweeter way to die.

Carefully, the cowboy made his way back to the opening to the surface. Being a little surer of himself on the return trip, he was there faster than he expected and wearing boots soaked with more spilled water than he'd had to drink that entire day. It was a nice change not to feel guilty about it, either.

The silhouette of Lizzy's curious face peered down at the cowboy as he reached the opening and he quickly held up the bucket for her inspection. "I brought it back in perfect condition, though I'm afraid it got a little wet while I was down there," he teased.

Those words had Ezra there in a flash and his hairy red hands hauled the sloshing bucket up like it was full of gold. "My God," he whispered as he set it gently at his feet. "It's so cold."

By then, the cowboy had pulled himself out into the open, taking a moment to bend over with his hands on his knees to get over the throw-up feeling from the sudden temperature change. He was just standing upright and brushing the dust off his jeans when Lizzy asked, "Can we drink it?"

Ezra, too, looked like a kid at Christmas waiting to hear if he could have a second orange. "I reckon so," the cowboy obliged the eager pair. "I had myself a healthy drink and I don't feel no worse for wear. If there's a finer drink of water within a hundred miles of this hole, I don't know where to find it."

The two hot and dusty settlers took turns taking slow deep drinks from their cupped hands, hardly believing that what they were drinking was real. When Scott assured them that there was plenty more to be had and no need to be polite about it, Ezra hauled the bucked up to his face and drank so deeply that it poured over his face and ran in rivulets all the way down to his elbows. After a few seconds of that he handed the considerably lighter bucket to his daughter and hooted a little victory cheer.

"Damnation! But if that isn't the sweetest thing I ever tasted!" he declared. "How far back in there did you have to go to find it?"

The cowboy, smiling as Lizzy fairly doused herself trying to imitate her father's method of drinking, turned and said, "If I had to guess, I'd say about a hundred yards. It's hard to know for sure, given how slow the going was at first." Thinking of that reminded the cowboy of the lantern he had been using, which he quickly snatched up from the dusty ground and extinguished.

Ezra frowned at the news. "It's going to be a heap of trouble hauling it out of there and then back to town, don't you think?"

"Yeah," the cowboy agreed, "but it'll do until we can find a good place to sink in a new well. I figure that if I can get back in there with some rope, I'll be able to get deeper in and track the flow. Assuming I wasn't too turned around while I was down there, it seems that the water flows right back towards Drum Hollow and was probably the source for the original well."

"That water weren't never so cold as this," Lizzy observed before wiping her mouth across her forearm.

"Could be that this here spot is closer to the source of the flow—like some kind of underground spring," the cowboy said. "It had time to warm up considerably by the time it reached the town."

Ezra clucked his tongue. "Don't know much about that sort of thing," he admitted. "But it sounds reasonable enough. What we need now is a wagon, some barrels, and buckets to haul the water up with. I think we'll be able to convince our good neighbors back in town to offer up what help they can."

Just then the cowboy offered the remains in the bucket to Windkicker, whose enthusiastic slurping erased any lingering doubt that the water was anything but pure. "I recommend hauling an old watering trough out here, too. It's going to be thirsty work for the horses as well as men, and what we take back in the barrels is going to have to be mostly for the two-legged members of the community and maybe some of the smaller critters like your chickens.

The cowboy made one more run into the cave to bring back a bucket to convince the town folk of their find. The trio set off on the return trip in considerably higher spirits than they had left the house with that morning.

Chapter Six

"Get on out of here with that nonsense," Albert fairly shouted when the trio reached town and entered the saloon. Most folks took refuge from the day's heat at home, but a hand full of townies and day-laborers counted on old Albert to provide them with something to fill their bellies with at midday. Those men looked on expectantly as the cowboy explained further.

"Look, the three of us and my horse have all drunk the water and we're feeling nothing but fine. There's enough down there for everybody, but it's going to take a little doing to get it out."

"Ain't nobody here got time for that," Albert explained with exaggerated patience and a brittle smile. Why the barkeep felt the town was his to control was anybody's guess but, since no one seemed keen on disputing it, he reveled in the chance to make a show of his authority whenever one presented itself.

"This is a town of working folk, not wandering cowpokes with nothing better to do than stick their noses in other people's business." Albert glared around the room to see if anybody would be foolish enough to speak out against him. "Ain't nobody got claim to that water if'n you found it where you say you did, not that we got any reason to believe that anyway, so haul up and drink as much of it as you want. Drink horse piss, if it suits you, for as much as I care for the issue."

Ezra stepped up, "Now see here, Albert! There's no need—"

The saloon keeper held up a silencing hand. "Don't you take that tone with me, James. The only reason anybody puts up with you in this town is because you got eggs to sell and that is all. More than once I've said we ought to have run you and your brat outta town well before you had time to throw up that eyesore of a shack that blights our fine community. I'll keep buying your eggs, since there ain't no others to be had, but I won't take any of your lip. You hear?"

The poor farmer backed down at the harsh words but the cowboy merely turned and spit. "If you're thirsty," he said to the room, "we've got water. It's cold, it's clean, and it's free. You're all free men in here and you can do as you see fit." With that, he turned his back on the bar and headed through the swinging doors to stand in the shade of the front porch.

"I'm awful sorry about that," Ezra said as he exited the building with Lizzy's hand firmly in his.

"No need to be," the cowboy said. He's brown eyes scanned the silent sun-bleached street. "Old Al in there don't need your help to be a horse's ass." He looked down at Lizzy and said, "Pardon the language, ma'am."

"But there's no cause for the way he just shooed us away like that. You said yourself that last night he didn't have water enough that he'd even take cash for it." Ezra shook his head in disbelief.

"I've met men like him before," the cowboy explained in a voice that sounded years older than it had any right to. "He's the big man in town and if there's water to be found, it's him that's going to find it. Anything else and he don't feel so big no more."

"So what do you reckon we do now?" Ezra asked, despair clearly on his face.

"We got your rain barrel. That's a start." The cowboy hooked a thumb into his belt and stepped out into the harsh midday sun. Once they were out of earshot of anyone in the bar he continued. "You know somebody else who ain't too pigheaded to give us a hand? We don't need a whole work crew, but another man or two would help. Maybe somebody who'd be willing to trade a little something for some clean water now and a chance at easier access later."

"What about Bixby?" Lizzy asked, tugging the edge of her oversized-bonnet further over her eyes.

Ezra bit at his lower lip. "Yeah. I reckon he's as likely a choice as any."

"What's his story?" the cowboy asked, his worn boots kicking up small puffs of dust as he walked.

"He's a rancher who's got a small herd a bit north of the water cave," the farmer explained. "He ain't what you'd call rich, but he ain't poor neither. I'm guessing that he'd be plenty interested in keeping his herd watered and he ain't got no reason to worry about Albert coming down on him for taking sides with us."

Taking sides, the cowboy mused. The idea that they were in the middle of some imagined feud made him uncomfortable on some level. "You friends with him then?"

"Not as such, but we get along well enough. He's fair in his dealings and don't speak bad of nobody." Ezra patted his daughter's head, "He even gave us book for Lizzy to learn her letters from."

81

Lizzy beamed proudly. "I keep it hid under my bed."

The cowboy nodded. "Yeah. This Bixby sounds like the man we want to talk to. Where's he been getting his water until now?"

"I can't rightly say," Ezra admitted. "It could be that he leads the herd to some little watering hole I don't know about, though he probably has his own well of one sort or another for the house. Still, I don't think he'd turn his nose up at a chance for more clean water—not with the weather being as it has."

"What say we take a little rest until the sun goes down a bit then," The cowboy suggested. "We can bring a fresh bucket with us and see if he ain't interested as you say."

Even with the door and both windows open, the shack was little better than an oven. Still, it was an improvement over being out under the unforgiving sun. More than once Ezra went out and used an old board to fan air through the chicken coop and keep his flock from cooking alive in their own little refuge. Though the death of the hens would rob the poor man of his main source of income, Scott had a feeling that his host thought of the birds more as pets than potential dinners. The cowboy might not have cared for their smell, but he had to admit that there was something comforting about the soft clucking and rustle of feathers that emanated from the building.

Later, when sun was hanging low in the sky, Ezra wiped the sheen of sweat away from his daughter's forehead. "Come on, pumpkin. Time to head out again."

The little girl yawned and stretched, her face settling into an unflattering scowl. She didn't say a word and neither of the men thought it wise to try to provoke her into speaking, either. Instead, they waited for her to lace up her boots and follow them out the door on her own.

The cautious optimism that had seen them off that morning had been replaced by weariness as the trio seemed more drained than refreshed by their afternoon respite. Only Windkicker seemed eager to stretch his legs and head off again.

The hour or so it took to reach the water cave passed in silence but the three travelers perked up as they had their second chance at a refreshing drink that day. The cowboy made two trips to the underground river to ensure that everyone had their fill and that there was still enough to impress upon old Bixby that it was in his best interest to invest in such a desirable resource.

Refreshed in body and spirit, the small group arrived at the Bixby ranch just as evening was settling in. The sky had darkened to a beautiful turquoise that lay across the land like a mother leaning down to kiss her child's cheek. The lovely scenery and stillness in the air added a sense of serenity to their mission and all of them felt glad, if still a little bit hungry, for their efforts that day.

The small cloud of dust the travelers were kicking up as they approached had alerted one of the ranch hands and he met them at the gate of the rough-hewn fence that marched along the front of the property.

"Ezra," the hand nodded, purposely avoiding eye-contact with the stranger until he was introduced.

"Duke," Ezra nodded back. "This here cowboy is called Scott, and we found something we think your boss'll be interested in."

The other man pursed his lips in thought. "Might be that he is, though I can't speak for him myself. What you want I should tell him you come for?"

"Tell him we got good clean water."

"S'that all?" The ranch hand seemed genuinely surprised. "He ain't gonna pay you nothing for that. I'll tell you that much for free."

"We ain't looking to sell it," the cowboy offered up. "We just want a little help getting to it. Once we done that, your boss is welcome to as much as he wants."

The ranch hand seemed to think that made as much sense as anything else he had heard that day. "Okay. I'll tell him you're here."

After a few minutes, a snowy-bearded man with a rail-straight back and a permanent squint etched into his face waved to the trio from the porch of the long ranch house. His clothes were of good quality, but faded by sun and infused with the grit of many an honest day's work.

"Mr. James," the man greeted Ezra. "I hear tell you want some help digging a well, or some such thing."

"Ezra," the farmer insisted, taking off his straw hat and holding it humbly in front of him. "If you don't mind. Don't nobody call me *mister* but you."

Bixby smirked, "So this is a social call then, being that we're gonna dispense with all of the formalities?"

"No, sir. We've made a find that we think you'll want to have a part in," Ezra explained. "This here cowboy and me found ourselves a good clean underground river

85

not far from here. It's raging fast even in these dry days and would be a good backup for you if'n you find your own well don't hold up so good."

Scott stepped forward as he was mentioned and stuck out his hand in greeting. Bixby didn't hesitate to take it and offered the cowboy a good strong pump as a greeting. "Pleased to meet you, sir," Scott said.

"You don't work for me, son," Bixby replied. "So there's no need of this *sir* business. Bixby will do me fine." The older man gestured for the trio to be seated in the chairs and benches that lined the porch while he himself leaned back against the railing just opposite. "And just what might you be wanting from me in exchange for the location of this wondrous hidden fount of yours?"

Ezra, clearly not comfortable speaking to a man he considered his better on a number of levels, was content to let the cowboy do most of the talking. Understanding the life of a cowpoke to some degree, the chicken farmer guessed that Scott was the veteran of at least a good handful of different bosses, and that he wasn't likely to be shy about saying what was on his mind.

Dark Rivers

"The water's free of course," the cowboy began, "but it's a bit of a chore to get down to it. I been in and out of there enough today to know that you ain't gonna have an easy time watering a herd of cattle, let alone a town from there."

Bixby nodded his understanding. "So it's a well you want to put in, is it? But of course old Albert's got the town turned against you so as you got no one to help you get the work done. That sound about right?"

Ezra was taken aback by how well informed the ranch boss was, but the cowboy seemed less so. "Some of your boys have lunch at the saloon today, did they?"

"Not as such, but we did get a delivery from a fellow that did. The way he tells it, you and Mr. James there went in with a fair proposition and he more or less threw it back in your face."

"More or less," Scott agreed. "I don't have no quarrel with him, but I'd still like to see to it that the town has a new well put in before I head out. Being that it was my fault the first one ain't good no more."

That information *did* surprise old Bixby. "You? How'd a scrawny fella like you bring on the quake that sealed off the well?"

The cowboy shifted uncomfortably in his seat. "That's a tale I'll share with you over a whisky some time—maybe two—but before that, I'd like to know if you'd be willing to spare a man and maybe a few tools to help us out. I reckon I can track the flow a little closer to town before we start digging, but there's still plenty of good water to be had until then. That is, if you don't mind the extra effort."

"That all you asking for?" the rancher asked as he scratched the silvery stubble under his chin.

"What about the wagon?" Lizzy muttered to her father.

Bixby's ears perked up at that. "A wagon?" he asked with false incredulity in his voice. "And what would a pretty little thing like you do with a big ugly wagon crashing and bouncing down the road?"

"We was hoping to haul some water back to town," Ezra spoke up. "Just to help folks out until we can get the well dug."

"That's mighty Christian of you," the ranch boss said. "Mighty Christian indeed. I reckon if some wandering cowpoke is willing to bend his back to help his neighbor, I can't do no less."

Ezra visibly relaxed at the praise. "I'm glad to hear it, sir."

Bixby nodded seriously and then turned his attention back to the cowboy. "There's details to be worked out if were gonna get this done in time to do anyone any good." He paused. "And I can't work out no details on an empty stomach." Rubbing a kink out of his neck, the older man made his way to the front door. After he took a step inside, he turned back to his guests and chided, "Well, get on in here. I don't reckon I'm gonna get any thinking done with all of your stomachs rumbling out here, either."

As the three sun baked and dusty travelers followed their host inside the sturdy ranch house, the cowboy decided he liked that Bixby fellow quite a bit already. He reminded him a bit of Henry Prescott, the cowboy's namesake, who had been one of the finest men the young traveler had ever had the privilege of knowing.

Chapter Seven

Dinner was a simple affair, laid out by Bixby's Indian housekeeper and wolfed down by a half dozen ranch hands in addition to the old man and his guests. What the meal lacked in creativity, however, it more than made up for in quality and volume.

There were fluffy white biscuits that steamed when they were broken open, a bowl of mashed potatoes as big as Lizzy's sun bonnet, and slices of pink, juicy beef as thick as a man's thumb. It was more and better food than the three guests had eaten in the past week and they set to it with gusto. It was clear that Bixby was pleased to see his guests eat their fill and he frequently instructed the Indian woman to pile their plates with more whenever it looked like they were in danger of finishing what they already had.

It wasn't long before the hands finished and wandered off to their quarters to spit, play cards, and otherwise enjoy the best part of the day. Bixby and his guests remained at the table and the cowboy was reasonably sure that if he had chosen to rise at just that moment he would have toppled over and rolled right on out the door. "You put out a mean spread for your guests," Scott praised and he picked a sliver of beef caught between his teeth. "Ain't nobody can say you don't."

Lizzy actually seemed to be in a bit of pain from her recent gorging, but she still snatched up the last half of a biscuit, glistening with melted butter, before the Indian woman could carry it away with her plate. "Why don't you take that bit of biscuit on out back and share it with old Moose," Bixby suggested.

"You got a *moose* back there?" Lizzy asked with eyes almost as big as her biscuit.

"Close enough," the old man said. "Only this one's got black fur and likes to run around barking at his shadow."

A grin spread across the little girl's face as she eagerly pushed her freshly plumped belly away from the table. "I hope he likes butter!" she called out as she headed for the back door, ducking under the arm of the Indian woman as she brought in a tray with three tin mugs and a kettle that gave off the heavenly aroma of fresh coffee.

"Thank you, Nan," Bixby said affectionately, patting the woman's arm as she set the tray down. "Why don't you go on and keep an eye on the little girl. It's a fine night to sit under the stars and enjoy a little time away from that hot stove."

Wordlessly, the woman exited the room and the three men sat in silence while the coffee was poured. Once everyone had a steaming mug in front of them, Bixby turned to the cowboy and asked, "It ain't whisky, but it's all I got on hand to loosen your tongue tonight."

Scott took the old man's meaning and he knew that he could not put off sharing his experience in the well forever. The young cowpoke took a thoughtful sip of the inky liquid in his mug, winced at the heat, and started in on his tale. There wasn't a lot of it to be told, of course, given that he hadn't been down in the well much more than five or ten minutes after all was said and done. Still, Scott included all the details he could remember and he never once apologized for how hard to swallow the tale might seem nor suggested that he was anything but stone cold sober and well aware of what was happening around him at the time. When he reached the end of his story, the cowboy took another sip of his coffee and looked out the window at the purpling sky. Though he hadn't been sure he was ready to speak as openly as he did, Scott felt as if a great weight had been lifted off his chest for having done so.

Ezra stared wide-eyed across the table at the cowboy as if he had just learned that he and his daughter had spent the whole day with a raving lunatic, but Bixby remained as stoically composed as ever.

"You are a brave young man," Bixby said after the silence had a moment to settle.

"I didn't know what was down there," the cowboy explained. "Nothing brave about jumping into a situation you don't rightly understand."

"That's not what I mean," Bixby replied. "Though it takes courage to face down that thing the way you did, too. What I'm talking about is your going down after that water today. Surely you must have believed that you might stumble upon some new horror down in that cave."

Scott fiddled with the handle of his mug. "I sort of tried not to think about yesterday, like it was just a bad dream. I guess in my heart I knew it really happened, but I just wouldn't let my heart and my brain talk to each other for a while. You know?"

The older man nodded. "I think I do. It's the same thing soldiers have to do to make themselves go back out on the battlefield after a day of watching their fellows get cut down. Ain't no shame in it."

"Are you telling me you that you are *buying* this story?" Ezra asked incredulously. "I mean no disrespect, sir, and Scott here strikes me as a fine man, but surly you don't believe that there was some demon in the well making the water bad."

"Is that what you're telling us, cowboy?" Bixby asked. "Is what you saw down in the well some demon done crawled up from Satan's fiery bosom to corrupt the fine God-fearing folk of Drum Hollow?"

"No, sir. I don't know what it was." Scott's voice was flat as he responded and if he felt provoked by his host's question, he gave no outward sign.

"See?" Bixby explained to his skeptical guest. "No one is saying there was a demon down there. Just...something. Are you suggesting that there wasn't something down there, Mr. James? That the well was empty when your cowboy friend went down there?" Ezra seemed taken aback by the sudden fire in the old rancher's voice and when the farmer didn't answer after a few beats, the older man's eyes dropped to the cowboy's wrist. "That where the thing bit you?"

Scott rubbed his thumb lightly over the scab-riddled area where little circles of skin had been ripped away by the creature's tentacle. "I wouldn't say bit, exactly, but yeah."

Bixby settled back in his chair and gazed into the gas-fueled lights of the chandelier that hung above the table. He seemed lost in thought for a moment though neither Ezra nor the cowboy made any comment. Finally the old man spoke, "I knew in my gut what caused the well to collapse," he admitted, "as sure as I knew the sun would come up in the east this morning. What I didn't know," he lowered his gaze to meet Scott's, "was that there was somebody down there when it happened. Once I learned that particular detail, I knew we had some talking to do."

Ezra, his expression as dumbfounded as ever, opened his mouth to speak when the old man held up a hand to silence him before he could even get started. "You're wise not to believe everything you hear, Mr. James, but you'd do well to keep your thoughts to yourself on this topic for a while. My pappy said that it was better people think you a fool for saying nothing than have you prove them right by speaking out of turn, and I've always been inclined to believe that. You just sit tight and enjoy your coffee a little longer and maybe you'll learn something new about the world."

The chicken farmer frowned but didn't seem inclined to argue. Instead he took a deep drink from his mug and asked, "You sure you ain't got nothing stronger than coffee?"

Bixby smiled thinly, "Not tonight I don't. Tonight I need a clear head to tell you something I ain't told no man since my pappy died some thirty odd years past. I told you I thought you was brave for going down into that crevice today, cowboy, and I meant it." He paused to lean forward and rest his elbows on the table as if he was about to being a prayer. "But I also said you was brave because you told your story and you told it true. There ain't a lot of men who wouldn't just keep it bottled up and tucked away for fear of being laughed at. I know I was. But sometimes a secret is just a story waiting for the right ears to come along to hear it."

"It was dry that summer, too," the old man began his own tale, "and I was a few weeks shy of turning thirty. My uncle Jim was having a coyote problem and he asked my pappy if I couldn't be spared to come out and help him deal with it..."

Bixby's uncle had a ranch a solid day's ride away and it would have been easy to miss it altogether the way the little settlement blended into the surrounding desert. If not for having the creek to follow, young Bixby would, like as not, have spent another day riding around in circles trying to figure out where he had gone off course. Instead, he arrived just after dark, dusty and tired, but otherwise no worse for the wear.

The air was cooling rapidly and carried with it the sweet dusty smell of hay and dried cow flops as the door to the house opened on the silhouette of a man with powerful shoulders and a round belly. Under other circumstances the figure would have been frightful to behold. As it was, he was a very welcome sight indeed.

"Any trouble getting here, Eddy?" Jim asked as he stepped out and took the reins out of his nephew's gloved hand. "You find the place okay?"

"Nothing different from no other day," the younger man replied. "The sun was a little rough, but I had this," he pulled his rifle out its long saddle holster, "for everything else."

Jim whistled appreciatively as the fine weapon gleamed in the lantern light. "Your daddy give you that?"

"Do I look twelve years-old to you, Uncle Jim?" Bixby asked crossly. "Pappy don't buy nothing from me no more, not even my excuses."

The older man grinned at the joke. "I hear you. And I'm glad you came. It'll be a big help to have someone who can handle himself with one of those. Only other fella anywhere around these parts is Andrews, and I don't think he could manage to hit the ground without a practice shot first."

"He here now?" Bixby asked as he removed his bedroll and began loosening the saddle straps.

"Naw. He's gone back to his wife for the week. I didn't have nothing for him to do and paying him takes too big a chunk out of my pocket as it is." Jim hung the lantern on a hook and helped his nephew hoist the saddle off and rest it across the fence.

Bixby gave the horse's rear end a sound smack and the beast started into the corral with an indignant snort. "Suits me," the younger man acknowledged. "I like to take care of things in my own time and not have to wait for some other fella before getting to work."

The two men went inside and settled in at the plank tabled that took up the center of the main room of the modest two-story house. A bowl with a towel over it rested in front of one chair, next to a chipped glass and a quarter-full bottle of whisky.

"That's your dinner, Eddy, such as it is." Jim pointed at the modest fare. "Ain't much, but it's what I got on hand. The supply wagon will be around sometime tomorrow and I'll see about rustling up something a little better then."

Bixby had already begun to wolf down the beef and bean stew, readily ignoring his uncle's tendency to mangle otherwise palatable food by being ham-handed with the salt. Before he reached for the whisky, however, he asked, "You got any water? It's been a dusty day."

Jim frowned, "Yeah, I got a little,though it's piss warm and full of grit."

The younger man put his spoon down and looked across the table, "What's wrong with the creek?"

"Dunno," came the simple reply.

When no further information was forthcoming Bixby asked, "So why ain't you drinking from it then?"

"The cows been dying from it, so I just been sticking to the rain barrel." The older man turned and spit into a battered bronze bowl next to his chair. "And you know we ain't had too much rain as of late."

"Pappy said you was having trouble with coyotes," Bixby said. "He didn't say nothing about the creek going bad."

Jim reached into his back pocket and fished out a small brick of sticky black chaw and offered it to his nephew. When the younger man declined, Jim bit off a chunk and began to gnaw at it thoughtfully. "No," he finally said, "I don't recall saying anything in my letter about no coyotes. I didn't pen it myself, mind you, but I don't think that fella who writes up all them letters at the post office would've added something like that without asking me first."

"Well, what did you say then?"

"I believe I just told him that cows were dying and I wanted your pa to send someone up who was good with a rifle." Jim spit again. "And that's just what he did."

Bixby pushed his empty plate away and uncorked the whisky bottle. "And what good do you think a rifle will do against a sour creek?"

The older man didn't answer at first, though his lower lip trembled just enough that a thin strand of brown spittle slipped out and beaded up in the black and grey nest of his beard. "Some things is just better discussed when the sun is up, Eddy." After that he would say no more. Luckily for Jim, his nephew was too exhausted to press the issue further.

Bixby woke up the next morning with blurry eyes and his shoulder pressed painfully against the stonework of the hearth. His uncle had offered him a bed on the second floor but the younger man knew it would have been a furnace up there. Why Jim had felt so inclined to build a two-story house was anybody's guess, but the most popular story went that Bixby's uncle had been smitten with a lady of a higher station and the house had been a failed attempt to woo her into marrying him. Though the accuracy of that tale was unverified, Bixby didn't feel it was his place to start digging into someone's private affairs just to settle his own curiosity.

"Let's get a little something in our bellies and head out," Jim said from near the cook stove, startling Bixby from halfway to full upright. "All I got is more of what you ate last night, but this morning you get to enjoy it cold."

The stew was thicker than the night before and beaded with white blobs of congealed fat. It wasn't the kind of fare that Bixby was partial to first thing in the morning, but he hadn't made the long trip north to enjoy his uncle's fine cuisine. It would give him energy to get through the early hours and that would have to be enough. "So you want to get started on the chores?" Bixby asked, wiping his mouth across the back of his wrist.

"Already done."

He found himself surprised by his uncle for the second time that morning. "What time is it?" Bixby asked. He was always good and tired after a full day of riding, but it was hard to believe that he had slept too long and too soundly to help out with morning chores.

"It's still early," Jim explained, "but I ain't been sleeping so well these days so I went out early and let you catch a few extra winks."

Bixby got to his feet and stretched the stiffness out of his shoulders. "No need for that, Uncle Jim. I came here to help you out and that's what I mean to do."

"I ain't worried about you earning your keep. You'll do that and then some before the day is through." And on that ominous note, the two men headed out into the yard.

Bixby's horse was enjoying a peaceful snooze, its pelt steaming slightly as the sun began the slow but inevitable process of turning a perfectly fine morning into a blistering furnace. "We going far?" the younger man asked. After the previous day's ride he thought it just as well to give his mount the day off.

"It's a ways," Jim answered, "but we'd be better off walking."

Bixby nodded wordlessly before adjusting the rifle slung across his shoulder. Whatever Uncle Jim was up to, he was taking his sweet time coming out with it. If he continued to be so secretive, the younger man decided, Jim could just go back and wait for that Andrews fellow to show up the following week. Family or not, Bixby didn't like being kept in the dark about the work he was asked to do.

"This way," Jim headed west towards the distant twisting line of grass and trees that marked where the creek flowed. The older man had donned a floppy farmer's hat to protect him from the sun and the effect was somewhat comical as it bobbed like a huge flower atop the rancher's powerful figure. "We're gonna follow the creek a ways and then I'll explain my problem. It won't do no good to try to tell you now because you won't understand it. So don't ask."

Bixby's belt, made of thick leather and heavy with rifle rounds, was already beginning to chafe against his sweaty lower back. It was a small matter, but it, along with his uncle's curt and seemingly condescending words, put him in a sour mood. If the water issue could be settled quickly, the young rancher was half tempted to start back for home that very day and apologize to his horse for it later.

The walk along the creek was peaceful, at least, but there was a conspicuous absence of animals for what was supposed to be a cattle ranch. His curiosity piqued, Bixby finally asked, "So where's your herd? I ain't gotten so much as the echo of a moo since we set out."

Jim didn't look back, as he thrust a hairy knuckled finger toward the north. "There ain't so many as there used to be, but those what are still alive and kicking are just over that ridge. You'd see them ready enough if we were going that far. They been a bit quiet as of late and I can't say as I blame them. Sometimes an evil wind blows through these parts."

"Just how far are we going then?" the younger man asked, intentionally ignoring his uncle's forbidding turn of phrase.

"Keep an eye along the creek bed. It ain't real deep right now so you can see a lot of rocks poking up." After giving his nephew time to turn his gaze towards the water, he continued. "Not far from here you're gonna see what looks likes the ground just sort of fell away and into the earth. I don't know how long it's been there, but I sure as hell didn't notice it last time the water was this low. Anyway, the creek sort of flows in and out of that space and any water downstream from there ain't fit to drink no more."

The younger man took note that the gnarly little trees and scrub brush along the banks began to look sparser and less healthy the closer the two men got to their destination. "So the cattle over the ridge are drinking from this same stream then?" Bixby wanted to know.

"Yeah, but they's fine so long as they stay north of that new hole," Jim continued. "I ain't willing to test the water myself, but it seems to me that whatever is turning the water sour is down in there and that's what killed a good chunk of my herd."

It wasn't long before the afore-mentioned break in the creek bed came into view. Bixby headed straight for it and squatted down to get a better look, being careful not to slide down the slightly crumbling bank. Not only did the gap drop down into the flat earth, but also into a large portion of the steep bank. It was only a few feet tall, but easily as wide as a barn door. The younger man could hear the water sloshing as it went in and out of the opening on its journey south.

After spending a moment to take in the situation, Bixby said, "So why don't you tell me why the hell you think a rifle is gonna clear this mess up. Christ on his throne, Jim! If there's something in there making the water bad, it's gotta be dead already."

Jim's face darkened further within the shadow of his absurd hat. "Don't you take the Lord's name in vain, boy, not leastwise where I can hear you do it."

The younger man frowned impatiently. "Save your sermon for Sunday, reverend. I told you last night I ain't no boy no more and if there's work to do here let's get to it. I didn't waste a whole day on the road to piss and fart about the weather."

Jim's expression looked as if he was fit to murder someone at that moment, but when he spoke again it was it was softly, almost as if he was afraid of being overheard. "Okay, Eddy. Let me give it to you straight." The older man stepped closer and draped a heavy arm around his nephew's shoulder. "There's something in there alright, and I guarantee you it ain't dead yet."

Chapter Eight

Old Bixby's hand had begun to tremble slightly as he reached that point in his story. He set his cup down and leaned back in his chair. "Woo-wee! I'd never guess it was gonna be so hard to lay all this out on the table." A sheen of sweat had formed on the old man's brow though the room was comfortably cool.

"You just take your time," the cowboy encouraged. "We ain't got no place else to be tonight."

"Speak for yourself, cowboy," Ezra spoke out. I got chickens that need tending to."

Bixby guffawed at the notion. "Them birds is sound asleep now and you full well know it. But if'n you're set on heading out, I'll be glad to hold the door for you."

His bluff called, the chicken farmer merely sat back in his chair and snorted his frustration. "All right, but Lizzy's gotta be in bed soon. She ain't no hen all snug in her roost now, is she?"

"He's right about that," Scott admitted. "I'm good with keeping campfire hours, but that ain't so for all the little girls on the premises."

"I tell you what then," old Bixby offered, "I'll lend you a good pony and you can take your daughter home and see to the chickens right now if you want to. It don't hurt my feelings none if you've had your fill of an old man's ramblings." Before Ezra could reply the rancher continued, "On the off chance you aren't in such an all-fired hurry to escape my hospitality, however, I'll see that you and the girl have yourselves a room in the big house tonight. That'll mean we can set to our task bright and early in the morning. You can take off then and see to your birds if it suits you."

"The *big* house?" Ezra asked.

"That'd be where you're sitting right now," the old man said. "The boy's call it that since that's where the big boss man lives."

"Speaking only for myself, I don't mean to go nowhere until you finish your tale," the cowboy noted. "That is, if you mean to tell more of it tonight."

"I reckon I do," Bixby agreed, "and you don't really strike me as the sort of fella who heads off with only half a story to keep him up at night."

As skeptical as Ezra liked to imagine he was, he, too, would not have been satisfied to head home before the story was finished. As such, it didn't take too much convincing to get him to agree to accept the old rancher's offer to stay for the night.

"I can tell you," Bixby, feeling a little more at ease for having taken a break in the telling, continued his tale, "that I didn't care much for how my uncle was carrying on. Something had spooked him, that much was clear, but I had the feeling that living alone in the wild had more to do with his peculiar behavior than anything down in that gap. It wasn't unheard of for folks living in them isolated homesteads to get a little soft in the head if they was given enough time."

Bixby continued his tale and it became evident that Jim did suffer a bit from spending so much of his life with only the cattle for company, as anyone would, but not in the way his nephew feared. The older man's head was sound and clear and he knew he hadn't imagined what he had seen a few weeks before.

"Eddy," his voice sounded hoarse as he explained, "There is something else down in that water. You might even be looking at it right now. It's shiny and black and it moves just like the creek. It's alive, I think, same as you and me, and I think it knows we're here looking for it."

Bixby wanted to argue, but the look of sincerity in his uncle's eyes robbed him of the spirit. Instead the younger man pushed up the brim of his hat with a gritty knuckle and scanned the water carefully. It was smooth in most places but a little choppy where it ran around and over larger stones. The bed of the creek was mostly white and yellow sand which shone brightly in the morning sun. Overall it looked clean and safe and just the sound of it made Bixby want to take a drink.

"So tell me what you saw again, Uncle Jim. It looks okay from here, but I gotta know a little better what I'm trying to see."

Jim cleared his throat before speaking. "I found this spot because those few head that died did so right here. Whatever is in the water killed them too fast for them to get very far from it. I found the poor critters with their tongues all black and blood running out of their eyes and arseholes. It shook me up a little, I ain't afraid to say.

"My first thought was that it was snakes or some such thing, but then I saw that the plants and all had died, too. The water was just as clear then as it is now and

I couldn't see nothing but rocks and sand until my eyes fell on that hole over yonder."

Jim let out a deep sigh before continuing. "I looked at that spot long and hard and I started to see something in the darkness. It was like another darkness, but deeper. I watched it slide and shift under the surface until I was sure that the sun must have been baking my brains."

Maybe it was, young Bixby thought, but he kept the notion to himself. "Did you see anything else? Legs? Fins? Some kind of eyes?"

"Nothing like that," Uncle Jim replied. "But when I threw a rock at it—" his voice began to tremble, "when I chucked a rock at it, the water seemed to boil up and I swear something big was coming to the surface."

Bixby was startled to see that his uncle was visibly shaking. The older man's arms were tucked against his sides as if he were suffering from a palsy. "What then? What did you see."

Jim's eyes looked dull and empty. "Then nothing. I didn't see nothing more. I just turned and ran." Then a powerful shudder ran through the rancher and he seemed to relax as his mind came back to the present. Taking a few steps farther away from the bank he said, "I come out here after that a time or two and tried watching that spot again and I *thought* I saw the same kind of shadowy thing again, but it was hard to know if it was really there or if I was just letting my yellow streak convince me that it was."

Jim absently reached for his wad of chewing tobacco, turned it in his hand, and then returned it to its pouch without taking a bite. "Once I even got close enough to touch the water with my hand and I felt something shift in the current. That seemed like warning enough not to try it again. Even though I couldn't trust my eyes as much as I'd like, I could still feel something wrong with the water. Not just with my fingers, you hear? I could *feel* that something was in that darkness looking back up at me. I had my gun with me that time, but I didn't want to shoot at it. I know it sounds crazy, but I didn't think one shot would take it down and I didn't want to be standing there alone when it came to prove me right.

"I'm ashamed to say I had Andrews do the moving of the cattle up north. I told him to stay clear of the creek, of course, but I think you can understand why I didn't say no more to him about it than that."

Jim Bixby was a strong and independent man and, family or no, it hadn't been easy to tell his nephew that something spooked him enough to make him turn tail and run right there on his own land. The solitary men of the plains took pride in their independent way of life and more than one fellow told tales of facing down storms and wild beasts with nothing but his wits and courage to see him through. Jim himself was known to readily share the tale of how he had handled a rattlesnake he once awakened to find nestled up with him in bed.

The veteran rancher was just as prone as any other man to jump at his own shadow once in a while, of course, but his nephew was finally convinced that there was more to the situation than just a lonely man who spent too much time out in the sun. The problem with the water might not be as terrible and mysterious as Jim supposed it to be, but the rancher was a wiser man than most for realizing that it was something best not approached alone. If it turned out to be nothing, then it was nothing and the two men would laugh about it over whiskey later that night. If it was something else, then Bixby would be damned if he wasn't going to stand by his kin and see it through to the end.

"Okay, Uncle Jim," the younger man began. "Ain't no doubt there is a real problem with this place and I mean to help you figure out what it is." When Bixby squatted and reached down to touch the surface, his uncle put a hand on his shoulder and held him in check. "I wouldn't," he warned.

The younger man let out an exasperated sigh. "You know I ain't gonna drink it and I got you watching my back if something in there starts moving. Whatever is wrong with the water, at least one of us is going to have to get a little wet before we figure out just what it is."

"Well," Jim conceded, "at least be careful then. The water might look pretty as a flower, but we can't go just by looks today."

Bixby nodded and reached out his hand again until his fingers slipped smoothly into the stream. The water was a little cooler than the morning air, but still surprisingly warm. The young rancher would have expected that kind of temperature for standing water, but a moving stream usually took a little longer to warm up. His pappy had always suggested that bathing in a cool stream was best not just to get clean but to wake up the whole body, and morning was the best time for it.

"Is the creek always this warm?" Bixby asked.

Jim shook his head. "It ain't, and I'm glad you noticed. You just take a few steps north of that gap and you'll feel the difference."

The younger man did just that and noted that the water upstream was indeed cooler. After pondering that for a moment, a new thought came to Bixby's mind. "There are places a little further west where hot water comes bubbling up out of the ground. It collects in pools hot enough to cook with, but you can't use it for cooking because it's all poisoned with sulfur or some such."

Suddenly the pieces started to fit neatly into place. "It seems to me that something like that might have opened up right here by the creek. That would explain why the bank gave away, why the water is warmer, and why it turned sour."

"Your daddy didn't raise no fool," Jim admitted after he reflected on the suggestion for a moment, "I'll give you that. But what about what I saw moving in there? That sure as hell weren't no hot spring."

"You said you saw something that looked like water, right? Something that we might be looking at right now? Hell, Uncle Jim, it might be that the water from the new spring is just a different color. The stuff I seen out west looked blue, purple, even orange in the right light. With the shadow

115

under the bank like that, shoot, I bet it'd look just like some nasty black thing moving around under the surface. All it would take is one big belch of hot water coming up from below and you'd swear something was rising right out of the water to swallow you whole."

Bixby rose to his feet and adjusted his britches where they had bunched up during his inspection of the water. The younger man had allowed himself to get sucked into his uncle's misguided, although understandable, fear of the creek and he was surprised by the intense sense of relief that washed over him for stumbling upon such a mundane explanation. Bixby wasn't certain, of course, but he figured that it was at least a theory they could test, and a completely sane one to boot. He thought that they might even be able to plug up the unwanted hot spring and set the creek right again, if that's all the trouble turned out to be. Making the stream safe once again, along with putting his uncle's mind at ease, was more than enough good to warrant the time and effort of having made the trip north.

Though he felt a reasonable amount of pride at solving the mystery of the poisoned water, the rancher's nephew did his best to hold that pride in check so that his uncle could save a little face. "If I was out here alone and saw something like that," Bixby admitted, "my belly'd be doing barrel roles myself, no two ways about it. It a damn shame about the water, of course, but, knowing what you do, if you just stay upstream of it, you ain't gonna have no more problems until we can get this all worked out one way or another."

The explanation was as sound and sober as any the man had ever heard, and Jim looked like he wanted to believe what he was hearing. Still, there was something about the situation that continued to nag at him. "I know about those hot pools out west," the older man explained, "but I ain't never seen one. You sure it's the same?"

"Sure I'm sure," Bixby assured his uncle. "I seen 'em myself and they're actually kind of pretty. They stink to high heaven though."

Jim looked at his nephew doubtfully, "What's that now?"

"They smell bad," the younger man shifted his shoulder under the weight of his rifle. "Something like rotten eggs."

"There ain't no smell like that here," his uncle noted.

"Well the *pure* springs smell like that. This one's being diluted by the stream. It probably smells a might worse over there on the opposite bank if you stick your nose right in that gap."

The rancher mulled that over and, not really finding any new angle to argue from, resigned to accept his nephew's explanation. "I do spend a little too much time alone out in this place," he admitted. "And a man does start to see things if he hears enough stories and spends enough time out in the sun." He scratched at his beard and his posture was considerably more relaxed than it had been just a moment before.

"Hell, I guess I'm just an old fool after all." Jim barked out a laugh that boomed across the open land, startling a distant partridge from its nest in the scrub.

Bixby grinned at the older man's new mood, "No more fool than the rest of us, Uncle Jim."

Feeling bolder, Jim approached the edge of the water and looked reflectively at the gap in the bank and the shifting shadows of the water within. "A hot spring," he mused. "Imagine that."

The younger man, now a few steps behind his uncle, asked, "By the way, what did you do with all carcasses?"

"Eh?" Jim turned to look at his nephew.

"The dead cattle. What did you do with them? If they was poisoned by the spring you sure as hell wouldn't try to eat them, right?"

A look of horror crossed the rancher's face as the question and what it implied struck him head on. Before he could answer, however, the inky darkness of the opposite bank suddenly boiled up and exploded into a nightmare of oily black flesh that enveloped Jim, snapped him backwards like a green branch, and drew him down into the water before he could so much as scream.

Bixby did that for him.

Chapter Nine

The old rancher's knuckles were bone white as the gripped the edge of the table. His voice remained steady, but it was clear that re-living the memory had taken its toll.

Ezra James looked on dumbly but the cowboy reached out and grasped Bixby's shoulder reassuringly. "That's good, old son. That's just fine."

"Nan," the old man called out hoarsely and the housekeeper was there so quickly she might have been a shadow on the wall.

The woman made a shushing sound before pointing to the little girl who was curled up on the black bear rug that lay before the hearth. The two had come in at some point during the old man's story, but the men had been too enthralled by the tale to even notice.

Bixby nodded his understanding that he should keep his voice low, though his expression remained pained. "Whisky, if you would."

The Indian woman shook her head in disapproval, but retrieved a bottle nonetheless. She set it on table with a look of distaste and retreated again to wherever it was that she had appeared from.

Uncorking the glass container with his teeth, Bixby took a deep swallow directly from the bottle. The rancher's eyes watered as the fiery liquid burned a trail to his stomach, though he did not shudder afterward. He offered the bottle to his guests and while Ezra shook his head, the cowboy took an appreciative sip to demonstrate his camaraderie.

"I guess I needed that after all," Bixby admitted through a forced grin. "I would have thought you did, too, Mr. James."

The chicken farmer shook his head. "No, sir. If I start drinking tonight I might start believing that tale you just told, and that is something I can live without."

"May be best if you do," the cowboy commented sagely. "Most likely it's something you'll never have to worry about."

"You got that right," Ezra replied. "I plan on helping you get started on the new well—I don't go back on my word—but even if the two of you are just as shithouse crazy as you sound, I ain't going to raise my daughter any place where stories like that are born. No offense intended."

"None taken." Bixby eased himself back in his chair, the whiskey already taking a little of the edge off his nerves. "No man could fault you for thinking as much."

"Whatever was in that well back in town," Ezra continued, "whether it was a hot spring, an animal, or the Devil himself, it already cost me my poor sweet wife and I don't plan on letting it take no more from me." It was a big decision to come upon so quickly, but, given the alternative, it was hardly surprising.

A quiet settled over the room as the three men sat pondering the night's events and the plans for the following day. After some time the cowboy asked, "I do have one question about your tale," he began, "if you don't mind."

"How did I kill it?" Bixby guessed. When the cowboy nodded the old rancher continued. "I reckon you already guessed the answer to that one."

"Yeah, I reckon I do."

After the silence stretched along a little longer Ezra finally burst out, "Well, *I* sure as hell didn't guess."

Bixby raised an eyebrow in surprise, but he explained in an even voice. "The answer is that I didn't. Whatever was down in that water, I didn't figure that my rifle wasn't going to put an end to it. More important than that though, there was no way for me to fire without fear of hitting Uncle Jim. I screamed and I hollered for a while, of course, but eventually the surface of the water settled and there was nothing to be seen but sand and rock and shadow again."

"You didn't even try to find him after that?" the chicken farmer asked incredulously.

The old rancher jumped to his feet, his chair falling back and hitting the floor with a bang loud enough to cause Lizzy to stir fitfully from her bed by the fire. "There was nothing to find, you damned fool!" He pounded a frustrated fist on the table. "And I was afraid. Just like good old Jim, I was afraid of whatever was in that water. I was strong enough to stand there and call his name until my throat was raw and my face burned by the sun, but I couldn't bring myself to go any nearer to those cursed shadows that day or any other." A sob suddenly rocked the old man's body and he turned away in shame.

Ezra and Scott were struck dumb by the sudden fury of the outburst. "Nan will see to your comfort," Bixby said without turning back. He shuffled off to his room without another word, seeming decades older than the strong confident rancher who had greeted them on the porch earlier that evening.

"What the hell--" Ezra began, but the cowboy shook his head to silence him.

"You can't fault a man for how he faces the darkness until you face it yourself," Scott explained.

"You faced it, didn't you?" the chicken farmer asked. "You didn't run."

"Like hell I didn't," the cowboy shot back. "The only difference between me and Bixby is that I came back again." He paused to stand and push in his chair at the table. "And who's to say I'm not a bigger fool for doing so?"

Morning dawned bright and clear again the next day and the men of the ranch gathered around to break their fasts on cornbread, eggs, and cool water spiked with mint leaves. Bixby arrived at the table late but, although he did not appear to have slept well, ate normally and spoke to his men with the same authority (and his guests with the same courtesy) as he had always done.

"Wayne, I want you to saddle up a pony for Mr. James and his girl to ride back to town with. I expect," Bixby turned his attention to the chicken farmer, "you'll be returning it with a fresh batch of eggs. I'd wager Nan used up our lot for this morning's feast."

Ezra wiped the stubbly corners of his mouth on his handkerchief and followed the hand Mr. Bixby had referred to as Wayne out to where the horses were starting their own day. As Lizzy went to follow, Nan stopped her and pressed a little napkin, no doubt containing an extra ration of cornbread, into her hands.

"Thank you, ma'am," the little girl said with a shy grin before she scurried out into the yard.

"The rest of you boys see to the morning's chores," Bixby continued, "And then I want the lot of you to move the herd to the east pasture and check the fences while you're out there. I don't want no losses like afore. I lose a single head this time around and it's coming out of all y'all's pay. Don't you doubt it for a minute."

"Kind of early in the season to shift the herd east, ain't it?" asked a gaunt faced man with a faded yellow bandana tied around his neck.

"I got my reasons," Bixby replied, and that seemed to be enough to satisfy the men. "Just leave behind those eight head we got marked for Dave Zierath," he paused to consider the number, "plus maybe one more on top of that."

Soon the room cleared out until only Bixby and the cowboy remained. Scott sat quietly, knowing his situation would be addressed in time and not wanting to press the rancher into doing so before he was good and ready.

After a long slow drink of water the older man put his cup down and looked down the table at his guest thoughtfully. "You still set on bringing that water up for the town folk and tracking down a site to put in a new well?"

"Yes, sir," the cowboy agreed. "That is, if you're still willing to lend your assistance in the matter."

"I like the way you come at life, boy," Bixby said. "I don't quite know what it is just yet, but I know there's more going on behind them Injun eyes than most folks. More because of that than because I got a whole lot of love for the town, I'm going to help you out."

The cowboy decided to accept the intended compliment rather than to correct the man about his heritage. "I'm mighty obliged to you then."

Bixby folded his hands on the table and explained further. "I'm going to send you and Wayne out with that wagon you asked for and let the two of you take what water you can back to Drum Hollow. You said the water there was good and cold and you don't look no worse for wear for drinking it yourself."

When the cowboy did not answer the old man continued. "That ought to take you the better part of the day. Then tonight, you, me, and Wayne can talk about what needs to be done for the well. I ain't needed a new one in a good many years, but I know how to go about digging one at least.

"I'm not in the way of paying folks who ain't working for me," the rancher continued, "and I wouldn't be much of a business man if I was. But I'll see to it that you've got a warm bed and full belly here on the ranch until this business is sorted out and you're ready to head off to wherever it was you were going before you stepped into this godforsaken mess."

"That's more than fair," the cowboy agreed. "But what about Ezra James and his girl?"

"What about them?"

"They've lost more than most by trying to make their home in these parts and something should be done for them. I've been at their place and I can tell you, Sir, they've got nothing to their names but their chickens and a heap of bad luck."

Bixby could not argue with that. "Last night Mr. James seemed pretty well convinced that moving on from this area was his best bet. That seems like the wisest course of action in their case."

"That it would," the cowboy continued, "and I think that's just what he means to do. Still, he ain't got no money and nothing but his hens to ride out of here on."

"You asking me to buy the man's chickens then?" the old rancher asked.

"It's either you or that ornery old fart Albert, and I trust you'd give Ezra the fairer shake."

Bixby sat back in his chair and considered the situation for a moment. "You're asking a lot of me, cowboy. I can't be responsible for every down-on-his-luck dirt farmer who blows through these parts." The old man's tone softened, "But I do feel for the man. I ain't had no wife to lose and no daughter to care for on my own, but, if I did, I hope I'd have the grit to keep going the way Ezra James has. He ain't the brightest star in the sky, but he's strong in his own way."

"That he is," the cowboy agreed.

"I tell you what. I'll talk to Nan about buying the man's chickens if he's inclined to sell them. She'll be sure to send him away with a fair deal. It'd be too much to ask for a pony, and I ain't got none to spare if it wasn't, but I can see to it that they've get some supplies and enough cash to get them on a coach the hell away from here. I might even have some old clothes to throw in to sweeten the deal."

"No one could ask you for more than that," the cowboy said. "And it would surely put my mind at ease."

"How you got this far in life with a heart like that is a mystery to me," Bixby commented. "Some might say that's a good thing, but someday somebody is going to sucker you with a sob story and take all you got to thank you for your trouble."

"Since I ain't got nothing," the cowboy grinned, "They're welcome to take all of it they want."

Chapter Ten

Bringing water up from the depths of the crevice was slow and unhappy work. Hauling bucket after bucket up and emptying it into the barrels on the back of the wagon would have been an exhausting task for a team of men, let alone just two. Both the cowboy and Wayne were content to work in silence, but they dusted off their hands and shared a few words at mid-morning when a break was in order.

"Where you headed after this water business," Wayne asked with a not unpleasant drawl. The two men were leaning against the wheels of the wagon, relishing the scant shade it provided.

Scott took a cool drink from the bucket that rested between them before answering. "I don't rightly know. I pretty much go where the work is."

Wayne nodded. "I used to live like that. It ain't a bad life, but it gets old after a while."

"That it does," the cowboy agreed.

"Bixby treats us fair and when I wake up with an empty belly I ain't worried I'm going to end the day the same way. That's a good way to be."

"Truer words were never spoken."

Wayne was a thirty-ish man of lanky build with thinning hair the color of old rope. He shifted in his seat on the ground and looked at the young cowboy thoughtfully. "You thinking maybe old Bixby will have a spot for you after all this?"

Scott shook his head. "No, I don't believe he will. But I can't say as I'd turn him down if he offered me one."

The ranch hand seemed satisfied with that and a silence fell between the two workers again. "They's together, you know," Wayne finally said after a while.

"Who?" the cowboy asked.

"Bixby and old Nan. They been like that for years, though nobody ain't supposed to know about it."

"Yeah?"

"God's honest truth," the man swore. "I heard Nan's people sent her away because she couldn't make no babies and old Bixby took her in. After enough time, nature just sort of did its thing."

"Who told you that?"

"People."

"What people?" It wasn't so much that the cowboy didn't believe his companion, but he had learned not to accept everything he heard as the gospel truth just because it was interesting.

Wayne frowned in irritation. "Just *people*, okay? Anyway, I had me an Injun girl once and I don't blame that old Bixby one bit if he turned sweet on his after keeping her on for all them years. Them redskins ain't all stuck up like the white girls who been to school and that. Talk less, too."

Bixby's taking in of a shunned and homeless Indian girl reminded the cowboy of how Henry Prescott had thumbed his nose at society by taking Scott's mother as a wife. It was further proof of the old man's character, if any were needed. Not having much in the way of a response to Wayne's story, however, the cowboy suggested that the sooner they got back to worth, the sooner they'd be finished with the god-awful task.

Noon came and went and soon the wagon was burdened under the weight of six half-full barrels. The two men had agreed that full barrels would have been too heavy for both the wagon and the horses that would be pulling it. What's more, half their haul would likely have sloshed over the sides anyway as it was jerked and jolted down the road. It went without saying that both the cowboy and Wayne were none too eager to spend any more of the day hauling buckets of the heavy liquid up from the bowels of the earth anyway, and the ride into town was a welcome respite for their empty bellies and aching shoulders.

"What's all this then?" Albert asked as he stepped out from the shaded porch of his saloon to investigate the arrival of the wagon. "I didn't order nothing from Bixby this week."

"It's a gift," the cowboy explained loudly enough for nearby folks to hear, "for the whole town."

Albert ignored the stranger and addressed his companion instead. "I'll ask you again, Wayne, what in the hell are you pulling into town with to get everybody all stirred up?"

By that point, a number of curious faces had peeked out of doors and windows to see what the commotion was about. It was early afternoon and although most people had been napping through the worst of the heat, the word *gift* piqued enough interest that a small crowd was slowly amassing in the road.

"Just what he said," Wayne replied, gesturing to the cowboy. Even if the two men weren't exactly bosom chums, the ranch hand didn't care for the way Albert disregarded the man he had spent the morning doing honest work with. "This here is a batch of clean cool water, least it was cool when we started off with it. Anybody who wants some is welcome to it. Drink it, cook with it, or give it to your critters, we'd be mighty pleased if we could take these barrels back to the ranch empty."

A happy murmur spread through the crowd at the news and a few people had already run off to fetch buckets and tubs when Albert shouted at them to hold on. "And just where did you get this water, may I ask? We had one well go bad and I don't see no reason why the same wouldn't hold true for another."

"This is from a clean new spring a good ways outside of town," the cowboy spoke up again. "We hauled it up ourselves and all the folks and beasts as been drinking it have been feeling nothing but better for doing so."

Once again Albert chose to ignore the speaker and address Wayne instead. "Well, you just take it right on back where you got it. I won't have you making these here people sick with nothing but you and some half-breed's word that it won't."

Dark Rivers

"Al," Wayne said with surprising patience, "This ain't your town and you ain't these people's keeper. And I *know* I ain't the first to say as much. This here water is as clean as the sun is hot and it's free to anybody who wants it. Anybody as don't want none ain't obliged to take any." The rancher's expression remained dull and he seemed fairly uninterested in any offense he may have given with his blunt words.

The saloon keeper sneered. "So be it, then. But if even *one* of these good people falls ill after this, I'll see that you answer for it." He turned his gaze at last to the cowboy and spat. "And maybe even hang for it."

The small gathering in the street seemed unsure of what to do as Albert wordlessly stalked back into his place of business. The cowboy, however, stood up and dipped a bucket into the barrel behind his seat and then took a deep satisfying drink from it. He filled it again, climbed down, and allowed one of the horses to do the same.

That was all the encouragement the group needed and soon folks were filling pails, wash tubs, and even empty whiskey bottles with the clean, clear liquid and carrying it back to their homes and businesses. Once the barrels had only a few inches of water in the bottom, the cowboy and Wayne unloaded them from the wagon and emptied the remaining contents into the saloon's trough. If doing so enraged Albert any further, he did not come back out to tell them so.

In less than an hour the people of Drum Hollow were feeling a might less thirsty and the two men who had brought the water knew without a doubt that their efforts had been worthwhile. With the empty barrels loaded back onto the wagon, the cowboy and Wayne headed into the cramped and aromatic confines of the general store where a round-headed man with thick black mutton chops sprouting from his cheeks waited behind the counter, sipping appreciatively from a pewter mug.

"Well if it isn't our saviors," the storekeeper said with smile as he adjusted the front of his green-striped apron. "What can I get for you today?"

"I'm gonna need a couple of pickaxes and about twenty-five feet of rope," Wayne replied.

"What are you fixing to dig up?" the storekeeper asked as he pushed his way through various supplies to track down the requested items.

"More water," the cowboy replied while thumbing through the pages of a penny-dreadful with a lurid cover image of a busty woman fainting into the arms of a man with a blazing gun in his free hand.

The storekeeper nodded as he counted how many times he had coiled a length of rope over his shoulder. When he was satisfied that it was about twenty-five feet he stopped and replied. "I figured as much. We're all mighty obliged for what you done for us today but it ain't gonna last us for too long. If we don't get ourselves a new well, and soon, this place will just dry up and disappear."

Wayne pulled out his pocket knife and asked, "You know anybody who might want to lend a hand with the work? The more hands we got the faster it's gonna get done."

The man wiped sweat from one furry cheek against his shoulder as he held out the rope to be cut. "There's always men looking for work, of course, but not always ones you can trust."

"Trust is important with work like this," the cowboy replied.

"And this ain't the kind of job that exactly pays anything," Wayne admitted. "Bixby is seeing to the supplies and mine and this cowboy's time, but that's all. Anybody else who chips in is doing so only for the sake of the water."

The storekeeper dropped the pile of rope onto the counter and looked at the two men. "That makes a difference then, doesn't it?" He took another long slow sip from his cup before continuing. "I can think of a couple of boys round here that ain't got much more than morning chores to keep them busy. I reckon their mamas would be happy enough to see their hands be a little less idle."

"We don't need no boys underfoot," Wayne explained. "Leastwise I sure don't."

"Digging a well can be dangerous work," the cowboy agreed.

"How about your Aunt Jesse's boy?" the storekeeper offered. "He ain't been doing much since he got back from the war a few months back and I'm guessing he's mighty handy with a shovel."

Wayne scratched under his chin. "But as I understand it, the bullet that earned him his discharge also left him sort of a gimp. He could barely stand on his own the last time I heard."

"Well, that must have been a while ago then, eh? He might not be quite the man he was before, but it ain't so as he can't work or nothing these days," came the reply. "Besides, beggars can't be choosers, they say."

A look passed between the cowboy and his companion that suggested that they agreed. "Okay," Wayne said. "We'll head out to Jesse's place as soon as you get them pickaxes I asked for."

"About that," the shopkeeper began apologetically. "I only got the one on hand, but I can order another one for you when the next coach comes through."

The ranch hand shook his head. "Naw. We ain't got time for that. Just give me the one you got and put it on Bixby's tab."

With their supplies packed into the back of the wagon, the cowboy and Wayne set off to Jesse's lonesome acreage a few miles west of town. It was a considerably more modest setup than Bixby's ranch, but the pens of sheep were neatly tended and the house looked sturdy if not luxurious. An older woman in a faded blue dress and dusty black boots was already waiting for them as their wagon came to a halt near the front gate.

"That you, Wayne?" she called out, craning her neck to see who else might be with him.

"Yeah, Aunt Jesse, it's me."

"Who you got with you there? He a Mexican or something?"

Wayne hopped down from the bench seat and the cowboy did likewise on the other side. "He's a hardworking cowboy, Aunt Jess, that's all that matters."

Jesse had not failed to notice the six-shooter hanging from the cowboy's hip and eyed the stranger coolly as she answered. "Mayhap," she replied without a great deal of conviction. "What brings you by?"

"I hear tell that Allen is back on his feet again."

"He is. If you came to pay your respects, you sure took your sweet time about it."

Wayne dismissed the intended barb. "I also heard that he might have a little extra time on his hands. I got a job that might relieve him of some of that."

The woman glanced back at the house. "*You* got work? Or do you mean that slave driver, Bixby does?"

"Now Auntie," Wayne explained in his singularly patient way, "he's a good man and he treats us right."

"Don't you *auntie* me! He didn't treat Jimmy right, now did he?"

Wayne frowned, "He tried to do right by Jimmy and you know it. A man sleeps in the bed he's made and all that."

Jesse harrumphed but let the subject drop. "So what is this work then? You know Allen's got a limp now, doncha? He can't be leaping over fences or any of that nonsense now."

Just then a rumble ran through the earth strong enough that the timbers of the front porch creaked and the horses whinnied uneasily. It lasted only a few seconds and was over as suddenly as it began.

"What in tarnation was that?" Wayne demanded.

Jesse frowned. "Just one of them shakes we get out here."

"We don't get them on the ranch. That's for damned sure."

"You watch that mouth of yours," Jesse chastised. "I don't know what you do or don't have out on the *ranch*, but we sometimes get shakes like that on this side of the town. They raise up a little dust here and there, but they don't hurt nobody."

Wayne looked to his companion. "You been around a good ways, cowboy. You ever been to a place with 'shakes' like that?"

"Yeah," the cowboy admitted. "They happen out in California all the time, but bigger, I suppose. When they happen there you can feel them for miles and miles, not just in one spot and not the one next door."

"Well, this ain't California, now is it?" Jesse snapped and turned to head back inside. "Now why don't you come out of the

141

sun for a while. If you want Allen to do some work you can darn well ask him about it yourselves."

Scott had met enough soldiers in his day to group them into three categories. The first kind were those who had been broken by their experience with war. Often those men were only shells of their former selves when they returned home and the rest of their lives were usually short and unhappy. Then there were those, like old Bixby, who chose to block out what they had seen and done as much as possible and go on with their lives as if that part of it had never happened. They did their best to convince themselves and others that they had not been changed and, sometimes, they managed to pull it off.

The third, and perhaps rarest, of the returned soldiers were hard men who had become only harder and stronger for their surviving their stint in hell. Like steel tempered in the hottest flames, those men had lived through the worst the world had to offer and had decided that there was nothing else for them to fear. Those were the men that often set off to climb mountains or shoot elephants, just to have another chance to face death and spit into its bony black eye.

While the cowboy had been worried that Allen might be that first type of soldier—a gaunt and jumpy fellow curled up in bed with a whiskey bottle clenched in his hand—that could not have been farther from the truth. Allen, with his short-cut pate and fierce brown beard, stood a hair over six feet in his stockinged feet and looked strong enough to lift both the cowboy and Wayne up, one in each hand, and toss them out the door if they wore out their welcome. He smiled as he firmly shook each of the men's hands with his own meaty paw, but it was a hard and appraising smile, as if being thrown out the door was the *best* the two men could hope for if they were not on their best behavior. Right away the cowboy knew that this was the sort of man who would neither back down from a fight nor walk away from one until it was good and finished. Despite the fact that Allen was a fella a person wanted on his side when push came to shove, it was likely that he would also be the one to have started the pushing in the first place.

"What brings you boys out here?" the big man asked as he eased himself into one of his mother's rickety wooden chairs around the dining table. "It's good to see you, Wayne, o'course, but I don't recall you really being much of the social type."

The cowboy sat quietly across the table trying to identify in just what way Allen had been injured, as the burly man had appeared to be the picture of health when he had risen to greet them.

"We're looking to dig a well," Wayne began. The ranch hand then went on to explain the situation as he understood it. His burly cousin listened patiently until the end.

"So you're looking for a strong back to help you with the lifting, eh? I can't say as I didn't get my fill of digging holes when I was with the glorious 47th, but I don't reckon it would kill me to do a little more." Allen cracked his hairy knuckles absently. "It'd do me good to do something besides tending sheep and listening to Momma warning me about how the gates of Hell is all but opening for me as we speak."

Jesse, working on some needlework by the window, gave her son a scathing look but said nothing.

"It would mean a lot to the town" the cowboy added.

"I don't give a hunk of dried horse shit what it would mean to the good folks of Drum Hollow," the former soldier explained. Though his words were harsh, there was no particular fire in his voice. "But with no water the town will fold up and with no town my sweet mother here won't have no place to do her sheep business. That's reason enough for me to pitch in."

If Jesse had been irritated by her son's colorful use of language, the concern he had expressed for her had washed it away. "Now don't you worry about me one little bit, Allen. I don't need no town folk looking after me."

"You got that right," Wayne admitted, "Aunt Jess is a tough old bird, but she's a darned sight tougher with you looking after her, Cousin."

The big man snorted. "And just who do you think it was as put the grit in my gizzard anyway?"

Eric Kerkove

Chapter Eleven

The cowboy, having the smallest build of the three men, sat in the back of the wagon as it bounced its way back to Bixby's ranch. It was already time for supper by the time they arrived, so introductions were made quickly and the barrels stored back in the barn with great haste.

During that time, the cowboy did not fail to notice the new feathery residents in the barn. Ezra James' chickens were clucking softly from within an otherwise empty stall. It was a makeshift home that would have to do until someone got around to hauling the old coop out to the ranch. Given what Scott remembered of it, it would probably be wiser to just build a new one from scratch.

Sitting around the table and breaking bread with Bixby's men was a familiar and welcoming experience to the cowboy. It had been a long day of hauling water and riding in the hot sun and food always tasted best when it was hard earned.

When the meal was finished, both Wayne and Allen headed out to the hand's quarters to enjoy an evening of throwing their money away at cards and bragging about how they were going to win it all back on the next lucky hand. The cowboy was about to join them when he caught Wayne's eye. The ranch hand nodded his head to alert Scott that his attention was still wanted at the table.

"You fixing to hang out with the boys tonight?" Bixby asked.

"I was planning on it, though I don't have no particular burning desire to do so." The cowboy hitched at his britches. He always felt a little naked standing around without his gun belt, but it was considered poor manners to sit down at the dinner table with a firearm strapped on. "You got something on your mind?"

"Just some questions. I won't keep you long," the older man replied. "Have a seat."

The cowboy sat down and looked across the table at the man who, just the night before, had shared a terrible secret. That admission had altered their relationship in an important way, but just how that change would manifest itself was yet to be seen. As such, the younger man waited quietly until Bixby was ready to speak.

"You tell Wayne and Allen about what you might find when you go poking around for water?"

The cowboy shook his head. "Not as such. I wasn't planning on bringing it up."

"Why not?" Bixby asked. There was an emotionless quality to the question that seemed contrary to the rancher's usual demeanor. "Don't you think it's something they should know?"

The cowboy frowned, wondering if this was some kind of test. "First off, I doubt those two fellas would believe me if I told them what I saw in the well back in town. I'd be lucky if they was still willing to work with me after hearing a yarn like that. Second, there's been hundreds or more wells dug in these hills and plains and I ain't never heard nothing about nobody else having trouble like you and I know about."

"So you figure that what they don't know ain't gonna hurt them. Is that right?"

"That's about the size of it," the cowboy replied. "You think otherwise?"

"No," the old man said as he sat back in his chair, apparently having heard the answer he had been fishing for. "I just wanted to see if we was on the same page is all. It looks like we are. You planning on wearing that on the job?" He eyed the revolver hanging on a hook by the door."

"Yes, sir." Scott hitched unconsciously at his pants again. "It's something I don't care to go without whether I got reason to think I'll need it or not."

The corner of the old rancher's mouth twitched. "Can't say as I blame you for feeling that way, but don't get so worked up as you draw iron and start shooting at shadows." It was odd advice from a man who knew very well that every shadow was not what it seemed. Eliciting no response from his guest, however, Bixby continued. "Now why don't you head on out and relax with the boys. But you get some sleep tonight, you hear? Tomorrow ain't gonna be no picnic. I'll tell you that much for free."

As the cowboy turned to take Bixby's advice, he couldn't help but think the old man had more to say. He turned back one last time. "That all?"

"That's all," the rancher's mouth said, but there was something vaguely threatening in his eyes that seemed to be saying a whole lot more.

Whatever thoughts were churning about in the old man's mind, the cowboy could not guess. As he made his way to the bunkhouse, Scott could only assume it had something to do with having shared a secret that might, should it ever get out, cost Bixby the respect of his men and eventually the community as a whole.

It kind of rankled Scott that the old rancher didn't trust him enough to keep his word without testing him first, but trust was something that wasn't worth much if it wasn't hard earned. The cowboy earnestly wanted to be in the old man's man good graces, however, and so he decided forget about the odd conversation and focus on the task that lay ahead.

Bixby was out with the men the next day, seeing that the well diggers had everything they needed and wouldn't be wasting time making any undo trips back to the ranch to pick up things they had forgotten. They had rope, pickaxes, and a couple of pulleys and some poles all strapped to the back of an ornery looking mule along with their other sundry supplies.

"Maybelle don't like to work too hard," Wayne explained as he cinched a rope around the animal's backside, "but we'll be glad to have her when the time comes."

"You go easy on her now," Bixby chided. "She eats half as much as you and pert near everybody likes her twice as much." The ranch hand grinned at that but added no reply.

"You reckon Ezra and Lizzy will be by today?" the cowboy asked. "I'd like to make my farewells if I can."

Bixby scratched at his neck. "Seeing as their business is done here, I don't reckon they'd come back here again, but you might meet them on their way out of town today. They said they was headed somewhere back east."

"I thought Ezra said he was set on seeing us get started on this well," the cowboy noted.

The old rancher nodded just before going into a short coughing fit. He pulled a handkerchief out of his back pocket and wiped what looked like a slight trickle of blood from his nose before continuing. "Oh, he probably meant to, but once Nan gave him his pay for the birds and loaded him down with biscuits, the open road must have been mighty tempting." Bixby dabbed at his nose again briefly. "Did you really think you were going to get a good days work out of him?"

Scott was a little taken aback by Bixby's question. While it was true that Ezra wasn't likely to have been as much of a help as the other men who had agreed to the task, an extra set of hands was always welcome. "Old Nan saw them off, then?"

"Yeah," Bixby confirmed. "The chickens was already here when I got back from checking on the boys yesterday but I don't blame them two for not wanting to stick around no longer than necessary. The future ain't getting no brighter sitting around on my front porch."

"I guess it's just as well that he not be underfoot," the cowboy admitted, though there was still a little bit of puzzlement in his voice. "You know, Wayne and I had the wagon yesterday and Ezra don't have no horse of his own no more. How did they get them chickens here on their own and how—"

Bixby held up a hand, irritation clear on his face. "Talk to Nan if you want all the finer points. I already told you I weren't here when Mr. James and his girl stopped by. All I know is that the payment I left for him is gone and the chickens are here. I don't need to know no more."

Without any further comment, the old man turned to go back to the house and the cowboy set off towards the horse pen to get Windkicker ready to head off. Questions buzzed around in the young man's head like angry mosquitoes, but he eventually resigned to the fact that he would have to talk to the old Indian woman if he wanted to know more and, besides, there was enough to be done that day that worrying about the travel plans of a worn out chicken farmer just did not take precedence. It was enough to know that Ezra and Lizzy, strangers just a few days before, were safely on their way to a better life.

There was something soft and reassuring in Windkicker's peaceful gaze as the piebald beast spotted his rider from across the corral. It reminded Scott that amidst the chaos and frustration of everyday life there were still good things—pure things—that were worth waking up for. There were treasures in the world that could not be bought with a mountain of gold, and the trust of a faithful beast was one of them.

"That your mount?" Allen asked, his large shadow falling over the cowboy from behind.

"That he is," Scott admitted as his horse came trotting over to him with undisguised enthusiasm as his companion hefted the saddle onto the fence.

"How'd a half-dried up tumble weed like you wind up with a fine animal like that?" the soldier asked. "I don't reckon he just followed you home from school one day."

The cowboy turned to judge the expression on Allen's face, but whether the soldier was serious or poking fun was impossible to tell. "I got him honest," Scott replied as he hopped into the pen in a display of agility that the burly, but crippled, soldier could not have hoped to imitate, "If that's what you're getting at."

Allen turned and spat. "I ain't getting at nothing, cowboy. I just like to know who I'm working with." He smiled a cool smile.

Scott's expression remained neutral. Allen wasn't a man he wanted to tangle with and it was too damned early in the morning for some kind of pissing contest. "That makes two of us, friend," the cowboy replied before tipping the brim of his hat slightly and turning his full attention to the half-ton animal that was nudging impatiently at his shoulder. It was going to be, the cowboy feared, a long day.

The three men and four beasts set off to the underground spring without fanfare, old Maybelle walking placidly beside the considerably smaller mounts. Allen's horse looked almost pained to be carrying such a large man, but there wasn't anything to be done for it.

Wayne rode in silence for most of the way, but there seemed to be no end to Allen's questions, once he got started, and the soldier didn't bother being subtle about asking them. For some reason he just had to know where Scott came from, who he had worked for and if he was Indian, Mexican or what. The cowboy had stock answers for just about everything, but his patience wore thin as the big soldier started asking about how many men he had killed and how that fancy bit of iron on his belt was made for men and not little Chinese water boys.

Wayne tried to change the direction of the conversation, but the soldier seemed about as interested in what his cousin had to say as he was in his horse's opinion on the matter. There was a hint of a smile on the big man's face as he repeated his taunt, but it was the mirthless expression of a bully trying to back his prey just out of the teacher's line of sight.

Scott was a patient man, but he was still a young one and there was fire in his blood the same as any other. "The day I need your advice on how to be a bigger man," the cowboy spat back, "is the day you need my advice on how to be a bigger asshole."

The smaller man's hands trembled slightly as he clutched the reins and Windkicker nickered as he felt the tension that was running through his rider. Almost immediately Scott regretted having lost his temper, but he knew he couldn't back down. The cowboy was no match for the soldier in a fistfight, gimp or not, but he had had enough of being poked fun at and shoved into the dirt as a boy to last another couple of lifetimes. He would be damned if he was going to put up with it now that he was grown and making his own way in the world.

Allen sat in shocked silence for the split second it took for the cowboy to brace himself for the coming battle, and then the soldier let loose a booming laugh that seemed to echo across the weed choked plains. "Alright," the big man admitted as his laughter slowly softened into a low rumble. "I guess I done rattled the cage enough to know what kind of animal lives inside."

"Weren't no need for none of that," Wayne protested. "I already told you he's a good man."

The mirth left Allen's face. "You'll pardon me if your word ain't exactly scripture to me, Cousin. If I set off into a fight I want to know who's got my back and whose back I'm watching and you don't find that out by asking the opinion of a man who met him just the day before."

Scott's eyes narrowed slightly at that comment. "What kind of fight you talking about then?"

The big soldier harrumphed. "I don't never wander out into the wild unless I'm ready for a fight. You got Injuns and worse coming out of every hole in the ground you come across and twice as many from the holes you didn't notice." He fixed his gaze squarely on the cowboy. "You mean to tell me that in all your wandering you ain't ever run into *unsavory* elements when you're making your way through these godforsaken lands?"

"I take your meaning," Scott said. He felt his blood cooling already and felt a little foolish for taking the soldier's bait the way he did. "The side iron I got ain't just for show and you can be sure I watch the back of any man watching mine."

"Good enough," Allen said, and the rest of the ride was as quiet as the morning was hot.

Chapter Twelve

The entrance to the cavern was just as the cowboy and his companion had left it the day before. All three men made their way down together, though they had to crack away a little more stone first to make the entrance big enough to admit the burly soldier, until they reached the edge of the rushing water which was just as fierce and cold as Scott remembered. They took turns holding the lantern so that everyone could get a drink and, after feeling more refreshed, they set about plotting a course to the most likely location to place the well.

"You know anything about digging wells, boy?" the soldier asked, his voice echoing hollowly from the dank cavern walls.

"Not as much as I'd like," the cowboy admitted, "but I figure we can track this here stream as close to town as possible and then start digging."

Allen snorted a big wad of phlegm out of his throat and spat it into the shimmering black surface of the water where it vanished into oblivion. "Well it so happens that I *do* have a little experience in that realm. I ain't no expert—make no claim to be—but I went along with my pappy a few times when he did it and I reckon I could do the same."

"Good to hear," Wayne said. "I'm just here to work a shovel."

"Your mama always said you'd do great things," Allen chided. "Now that I can see which way the water is going, I'm going to try my hand at a bit of dowsing. You know about that, cowboy?"

The word sounded familiar, but Scott couldn't quite place where he had heard it before. Then an image popped into his mind from an old tintype he had seen somewhere at the Prescott ranch. "Is that were you try to find water with a stick?"

"Ah-yeah," the soldier agreed. "That's the pretty much the long and short of it."

"So what do you do with the stick?" Wayne asked as they started to make their way back to the surface. "You poke at the ground until you hit water."

Allen snorted. "You'd need a damn long stick for something like that. No, I'm just going to hold the stick and it's going to point the way to the wet stuff."

Figuring that he was the butt of some kind of joke, Wayne let out a chuckle. "Okay. Then, when you find it, I'll point the shovel at the ground and it will start digging for me, too."

The soldier scowled at his cousin's ignorance, but it was too dark for the thinner man to notice. "Just watch and learn," Allen grumbled.

"Well, shit! You sound like you're serious."

"He is serious," Scott explained. "I ain't never seen it done myself, but I've read that it can be."

"Like reading, do ya?" The soldier asked as the three men begrudgingly exited the comfortable confines of the cavern and back into the unforgiving sun. Almost immediately their cool skin beaded with fresh perspiration.

"When I can," the cowboy admitted. "Though that ain't as often as I'd like."

Allen crossed his arms in front of his broad chest, "Well ain't you just full of surprises. What would you call your favorite book, then?"

"It's a hard call, but I'd probably say *Wuthering Heights*. I used to keep a copy in my saddlebag, but it got stuck to somebody's fingers and walked off one day." The cowboy stretched a kink out of his shoulder. "You heard of it?"

"Course I heard of it," Allen barked back. "And that's a woman's book if I ever read one."

The cowboy grinned, "So you're saying that you read it, eh?"

Allen started rummaging through the pack strapped to the side of his horse. "I ain't saying as I didn't, just that it ain't fit to be no man's favorite."

"And what *would* be fit, then?" Scott asked.

"*Bootstraps and Blood*, for one." Allen explained as he closed the flap of one pack and starting poking through another. "It's got better fistfights than *Wuthering Heights* and half the damn characters don't die of consumption."

Chuckling, the cowboy conceded. "I'll take your word for it. If I come across a copy I'll be sure to give it a read."

"I'll lend you mine," the soldier said as he found what he was looking for. "It's back at Mama's place for the moment."

"That your drowsy stick," Wayne asked as he saw the thin Y-shaped object in his cousin's hand.

"It's a *dowsing rod*, Wayne. If there was such thing as a drowsy stick, I'd imagine you been hit with it one too many times."

Eric Kerkove

The ranch hand took the ribbing as
good naturedly as ever and Scott couldn't
help but wonder if the man wasn't a little too
laidback for his own good. Still, not just
anyone could get along with Allen and it was
one less worry knowing that the two cousins
weren't going to start going at each other
over a jibe here or there.

"So what do you need us to do?" the
cowboy asked.

"Just stay back," Allen ordered, the
soldier coming out in his voice more than
ever. "I need you boys to give me a wide
berth so I can feel the energy in the ground."

Wayne took his hat off just long
enough to scratch his head. He could not
have looked more confused had his cousin
suggested he was going find gold with a
boiled carrot, but he decided to just stand
aside and do as he was told. Allen was, in
general, a decent fellow, but when his mind
was set on a task, a man took his life into
his own hands if he got in the way.

The big soldier stood with his feet
shoulder-width apart and one beefy hand on
each of the rod's thin protrusions, the way a
farmer might hold onto a tiny plow. There
was no wind at the moment and the sun
beat down on man and beast alike, adding a
heavy almost palpable feel to the tension in
the air. The front tip of the dowsing rod

bobbed slightly when Allen shifted his weight away from his gimp leg, but otherwise seemed in no hurry to lead the man to water.

Wayne watched in his relaxed way, but there was a hint of anticipation in his eyes. The cowboy, however, was watching so intently that he actually jumped a little when Windkicker pawed impatiently at the ground behind him. One minute turned into two and then five, but the soldier didn't move and his companions didn't dare make a sound until asked to do so.

"Well, shit," Allen muttered, dropping his fatigued arms back to his side. "Maybe I ain't doing something right."

"Could be that you're just too tense," the cowboy offered.

"Come again?"

"Well that's a pretty tiny stick you got there but you're holding it out like your trying to tell *it* where the water is." Scott shrugged, "Just a thought."

The corner of Allen's mouth twitched in irritation, a barely visible gesture beneath his beard, but one that the cowboy did not fail to notice. The soldier was about to offer an unappreciative reply when Wayne suddenly spoke out.

"Well, will you look at that!" The lanky ranch hand stretch out a finger to point at his cousin's arm. The burly limb was swinging slowly by the big man's side in a subtle pendulum motion.

Allen looked down and was surprised himself. Without otherwise changing his posture, the soldier watched as the arc of his own arm's momentum increased until it was swinging as wide and steady as a clock. A look of fascination dawned across his face.

"I'll be damned," the big man said as he turned and started heading in a line away from the cavern entrance, allowing his arm to swing freely and guide him west into the rough.

The cowboy and Wayne let him make his way a few dozen yards ahead of them before they took up the animals and began to follow slowly behind. No one spoke for fear of breaking the spell that seemed to have fallen over the soldier and his dowsing rod. Even Maybelle seemed to respect that something special was happening and allowed herself to be lead as gently as an old woman crossing the street.

The group walked that way for the better part of thirty minutes, Allen making his way slowly to the northwest. At one point he paused and took the risk of holding the dowsing rod in the traditional manner and, thankfully, still seemed to find that familiar pull. The difference, as Scott noted to himself, was that the man's powerful arms were much more relaxed than when he had first tried to get the feel for the device. Allen now held the stick loosely like the reins of a horse that was headed in the right direction rather than something that was trying to get away from him.

About three-quarters of a mile north east of the nearest visible Drum Hollow building, the big man simply stopped moving forward and waited for his companions to catch up. "This is the spot," he declared with no further explanation. The dowsing rod was pointing straight down to the spot between Allen's feet. The big soldier couldn't say exactly how he knew that he had found the right spot any more than he could explain how the rod had led him that far in the first place, but something about it just felt right.

"Let's get to work then," Wayne declared. Digging a hole was a concept that the ranch hand could readily grasp and he was ready to get to it. He would leave the mysterious workings of the *drowsy stick* to be pondered by men sophisticated enough not only to read books, but to do so for pleasure.

The three workers secured the horses and methodically set to unloading Maybelle. They scratched out where and how wide they wanted to dig by dragging their boot tips in the hardpan. Few words were exchanged as each man performed his task without first needing it explained to him.

Allen took the first great swing with his pickaxe, no doubt eager to see if his intuition was right, driving the heavy tool deep into the hard soil and ripping it back up in a satisfying spray of reddish earth. Wayne followed suit with his own until the two cousins were working back and forth as smoothly as men on a railroad handcar. Knowing it would take a few minutes before either of the two was tired enough to be relieved, the cowboy began scouting the area for stones large enough to circle the well with.

Ideally they would have brought materials to mix up mortar and built a ringed wall around the well. Without one, anything could (and likely would) fall in and pollute what was hopefully a pristine offshoot of the stream back at the cavern. But the three men had had limited time to plan and even less experience to judge by and so they had come as prepared as they thought necessary. There would be time to smooth out any rough edges, the cowboy knew, and the important thing was to safely reach the water. Anything else was secondary at that point.

There weren't a lot satisfactory rocks to be found in the vicinity, so Scott wandered gradually away from the other men until he came upon a bald spot in the scrub scattered with bread loaf-sized stones too uniform to have occurred naturally. *Somebody built* something *here before*, the cowboy mused, but he would be darned if he knew what it might have been. Still, he hefted a couple of the weighty stones under his arms and returned to the diggers with them.

Allen paused in his efforts and wiped his brow as the cowboy approached. "Find many more of those?" he asked.

"Enough, I reckon." Scott dropped the rocks near the pile of earth the two diggers had already dredged up. "There's a good number of them just over yonder." He pointed to the area he had just come from. "Used to be a house or something there."

The soldier eyed the building stones. "Most likely. Why don't you keep bringing them over while we stick to this. We'll need your help once we get to using the mule and pulley, but that ain't going to be for some time."

Allen and Wayne went back to their rhythmic swinging and clearing of the hole while the cowboy carried stones back in sets of four. It wasn't until he had carried more

167

than two dozen of the rough-hewn rocks back that he noticed a few of them appeared to be engraved with some sort of markings. He made the discovery when he felt his thumb slide into a groove on one. A puff of breath was enough to clear the dust out of it.

What was underneath was a deep curved line that began in roughly the lower center of the stone and ran to the opposite end. Further searching turned up stones with similar markings but they were all too broad and simple to resemble the written words he initially thought they might be a part of. Scott wondered if perhaps they formed a picture and the challenge of discovering if that was true appealed to him greatly. The cowboy lamented that there was no time for such games, but he decided to leave any stones with markings on them behind, moving only those that were completely plain. When they broke for lunch, he decided, he would come back and investigate further.

By the time the sun was at its highest point in the sky, Allen and Wayne were covered in muddy mix of red dust and sweat. Their hands were caked over at the knuckles and more than one finger sported a garish smear of blood from a clearing a sharp stone. Though the square hole they dug was only about three feet deep, both men were good and ready to put down their tools and savor the sweet taste of biscuits, jerky, and piss-warm water. It might not have looked like much of a feast to passersby, but it was hard earned, by God, and that made it a feast like no other.

There was precious little shade to be had and most of that came from a careful positioning of hat brims, but a little water cooled the throats and loosened the tongues of the three men as they enjoyed their time relaxing on the bottoms of overturned buckets.

At first, the talk was limited to how the work was going and how much of it was left. Wayne was hopeful that they could complete the work before dark while Allen was less optimistic. Since they didn't know how far below the water lay, they had little more than guesswork to judge by, which, they all agreed, was a less than satisfying way to go about a job. The cowboy thought that the strength of the dowsing rod's response suggested that the water might be closer to the surface than they feared, though Allen had no basis of comparison to either accept or reject the notion.

When there was a pause in the conversation, Scott stood up and stretched the tightness out of his back. His eyes

169

wandered over to the area where he had found the brick-shaped stones for a moment while the wheels of his mind turned thoughtfully. The young wanderer pondered over what kind of structure might have one been there and what the markings on the stones might mean.

"Something over there, cowboy?" Allen asked, his gaze following to where Scott was looking.

"Just wondering what might've been built back where I found them stones. I didn't see nothing like a building foundation, but they had to have been part of something at some point."

"Maybe it was a grave," Wayne offered.

The cowboy looked down at his ranch hand companion in surprise. That thought had never even occurred to him. "Yeah," he agreed. "It could've been at that."

"Maybe it's an old Injun burial place," Wayne continued, "full of treasure or something."

"When the hell was the last time you saw some Injun hauling around a load of treasure?" Allen reproached his cousin. "I can't help but wonder if there's anything really going on between your ears or if it's just full of dust and cobwebs."

"Maybe we ain't never seen no Injun treasure," Wayne explained, "because they got it all buried in places like out here." The lanky man looked especially pleased when his cousin could do no more than roll his eyes and snort as a reply.

"Whatever it was, it might've been important," Scott offered. "Some of them stones got marks on them and I think they might make some kind of picture if we put them all together."

Allen's curiosity was piqued. "Is that right? Maybe it makes the shape of an eagle or some such thing."

"I know we ought to be getting back to work here, but I can't say them stones wouldn't be nagging at the back of my mind if I didn't give them another look while I've got the chance." The cowboy looked from his companions faces back to where the stones lay. "You fellows want check them out for a bit?"

Allen might have been an uncouth brawler on the outside, but he still had a lot going on upstairs. Much like the cowboy, he could not resist the idea of investigating some ancient puzzle left out in the middle of the plains. "I don't suppose sparing a few minutes would put us too far behind," the big man said more to himself than to the others.

171

The three headed over to the clearing in the brush and looked down at the scattering of stones that the cowboy had left behind. Some of them contained only a single curved line while others were more complex in nature.

"I'm guessing that some of them form a circle," Scott explained. "I think if we put that together first, we might be able to see if the others don't fit inside."

Without further hesitation the trio began pushing the stones around and turning them to see if they didn't come together in one way or another. Occasionally one man would ask another for the one in his hand but they otherwise wordlessly found the pattern through trial and error and within a few minutes had constructed a surprisingly regular shape. The stones themselves rested against each other in a horizontal fashion, as they would in a brick wall, but the single unbroken groove formed by them was a near perfect ring.

It became a more complicated endeavor after that, however, as the rest of the engravings did not seem to fit together in any discernible way. Some of the bricks seemed to connect but trying to make those partial shapes fit with the rest of the image was nigh impossible. Whatever the picture the lines were intended to make, it wasn't something that any of the three men recognized.

"I guess it must just be some pattern," the cowboy said with resignation in his voice. "All of these swirls and such look like something I saw on some Mexican blankets once, though I was kind of hoping it might be a person or an animal or the like."

Allen nodded, "Yeah, I don't think we're going to figure it out just standing here while the sun bakes our brains. Let's get back to work and maybe we can come back to it later."

Though his words were civil enough, the cowboy could tell by Allen's posture that the big man was not happy to be beaten by anything, even if by just a bunch of dusty rocks out in the middle of nowhere. Wayne, too, sensed the tension and so all three headed back to the animals with no further discussion of the stones and their ancient cryptic meaning.

After they had been watered, the horses seemed more than content to be left to their own devices and munch on scrub grass while the humans played in the dirt. Maybelle, on the other hand, was ready to work. Whenever she left the corral, she expected to carry or pull something and the impatient way she flicked her long dark ears showed that she itched to get to it.

Allen and the cowboy used some old bamboo poles and twine to build a teepee shape to hold up the pulley while Wayne secured one end of the new rope firmly around the mule's midsection in an effort to make the most of her pulling power. Although the ranch hand might not have been the most brilliant speaker he had ever met, Scott had to admit that Wayne knew how to handle animals. It wasn't just anyone who could get a beast as powerful as Maybelle to be so docile while she was trussed up for the coming job.

It was maybe 30 minutes of work to get the entire operation the way they wanted it, but the time and effort the pulley rig would save, not to mention the aching muscles it would avoid, would be well worth it. At least that was how it played out in the minds of the men who had gone to all the trouble of setting the rig up.

The system was fairly simple. Allen and the cowboy would step back into the hole and continue to dig with a couple of small shovels that the soldier had scavenged after the war, while using the pickaxes to break up any large stones they came upon. Rather than try to haul the heavy debris out by hand, however, they would load it into a bucket, at which point Wayne would lead the mule to pull it to the top and then dump it to the side. With any luck, they'd reach moisture before dark and perhaps be able to break clean through into the stream they envisioned was waiting below.

The work went along as planned for a few solid hours with only basic grunts and gestures for communication. There just wasn't enough steam in a man's engine to spare on idle chatter and the closer they thought they were to the water, the more doggedly determined they were to reach it. The sun was hanging considerably lower in the sky when the tip of the cowboy's shovel struck hard enough against a buried stone to jar his shoulder and rattle his teeth a little. By that point, the lip of the hole was shoulder-high and it was getting difficult for the two men to work side by side and so the cowboy had to be careful about how he tried to excavate the stone if he wanted to avoid being banged in the head by Allen's hambone-like elbows.

"This looks like a big one," Scott offered after he grew frustrated enough to need a break. "I've been poking around at it for a while and I ain't found the edge yet."

Allen harrumphed and started clearing away the area closest to the cowboy's boots until he found what the other man had been talking about. "This is mule's work if I ever saw it," he eventually agreed as he rested his forearms on the hand of the shovel's handle and considered their options. "We might as well get it ready for her unless you think she's going to squeeze down in here with us."

After a few more minutes of clearing away the soil, it became obvious that the two workers were standing on a large slab of rock, only part of which had been uncovered by the cowboy. The rest of the stone was still buried in the side of the dig and had to be cleared out for another foot before the opposite edge was uncovered.

"What the hell is this?" Allen asked no one in particular. The stone they uncovered was too regular in shape to be natural and appeared to be made of the same rock as the engraved bricks the cowboy had discovered nearby.

"Could be the foundation of a building," the cowboy said. "If there was one building nearby, why not two?"

"Might be a grave," Wayne offered up again. Although it was the same suggestion as had made earlier, it was considerably more unsettling under the current circumstances.

The cowboy was sure that Allen was going to lash out with his sharp tongue, but the big man simply hauled himself out of the hole in a single thrust of his muscular arms. "Whatever it is," he said as he brushed earth from the knees of his pants, "it's in our way."

The soldier handily untied the bucket at the end of the pulley and dropped the slack rope down into the hole. "Now, you secure your end down there and we'll see if we can't get the mule to loosen it up a bit. I doubt she'll pull it out in one go, so we'll just take it one step at a time."

The cowboy did as he was instructed and, once he felt the stone was tied as securely as he could get it, joined the other men back by old Maybelle."

"You do it right?" the soldier demanded, giving the rope a solid jerk to see if it would hold.

"Yes, sir." Scott confirmed. He was getting used to the soldier's brusque way of going about a job and didn't feel he could fault a man for being ornery as long as he was willing to do his share of the work. "It's all up to Maybelle now."

"C'mon girl," Wayne said in his softly encouraging voice. The mule's back was to the hole as she took her first few steps away until the rope pulled taught. "That's the way now. Keep ah goin'."

At first, it looked like the stone wasn't going to budge even an inch as the mule's muscles strained and the tendons in her neck tightened. Then the great animal dropped her head for a moment as if to focus her effort and with a mighty tug she jerked forward. A crack like a gunshot boomed from inside the hole as the stone broke in half, startling man and beast alike.

Immediately, the cowboy and Allen rushed to the edge of the pit to see how the stone had broken and whether or not it seemed likely that the mule would be able to pull out the fragmented chunk without having to secure it again. Before they reached it, however, the earth began to tremble violently the way it had at Aunt Jesse's farm the day before. The two men stumbled and went to the ground as the horses whinnied in terror. Maybelle lunged so fiercely away from the dig that the piece of stone she was tied to jumped into the air and smashed the pulley system to kindling.

The weight of the rock, however, pulled it right back down and suddenly Maybelle was being dragged backwards towards the hole, her head thrashing in protest. Although the earth became still just as quickly as it had erupted into motion, all three men were too stunned to immediately realize what was happening.

"Cut the rope!" Wayne screamed as soon as he saw that Maybelle's rear hooves were only a few inches from the edge of the hole. The ranch hand's face was slack with horror as his mind's eye envisioned the powerful animal falling into the hole and disappearing into some unknown darkness below.

The great mule struggled with all the power her panic-filled loins could muster, but it was all she could do to hold her ground for the few precious seconds it took Allen to pull free the huge knife that hung from his belt. With surprising speed and accuracy, the soldier hacked through the taut rope like an axe splitting firewood, setting the mule free just a fraction of a second before the ground at the lip of the pit crumbled inward.

Maybelle stumbled forward as the tension broke and then bolted off into the plains in the general direction of the ranch. Behind her, she left a trail of dust and the scattered few items that had still been strapped to her sides.

The cowboy's heart was pounding in his chest in time with the sound of the receding hoof beats as he got back to his feet. So much unexpected and potent violence had come out of nowhere and it was a miracle that no one had been crushed or trampled amidst the chaos.

"That mule was damn lucky," Allen said, pointing the tip of his knife into the hole.

Both Wayne and the cowboy approached on shaky legs and peered down in what had been a fairly shallow hole only a moment before. Now it was a gaping maw in the earth with the sound of water rushing up from deep down in the blackness below.

Dark Rivers

Chapter Thirteen

"It don't make no sense," Wayne continued to argue. "That chunk of rock weren't so big as to pull Maybelle back like that. Hell, you saw her jerk it clean into the air afore it dropped back in."

"She was spooked is all," Allen informed his cousin. "She probably just froze up with fear. I've seen it happen to enough men in my time."

"But I know—" Wayne started before he saw the cowboy shaking his head. Allen was as unsettled by what had just happened as anybody, but his way of dealing with the situation was to forget about what they didn't understand and keep moving forward with what they did. It was the soldier's way.

"She going to be okay out there?" The cowboy asked. He nodded his head in the direction the mule had fled.

"I don't doubt it," Wayne admitted. "She might be stubborn, but she ain't stupid. If I had to wager, I'd say she'll make her way home and will be there a damn sight sooner than the rest of us. Still, it won't

181

hurt to keep an eye out for her when we head back."

"I reckon that might as well be sooner than later," Allen said with his meaty fists planted firmly against his hips. Though the soldier would not have admitted it, it was clear that the day's work had taken its toll and his body was hurting more than the other two could fully understand. "All our gear is shot to shit now so we might as well pack up and finish this off right tomorrow instead of doing some kind of half-assed job today."

The cowboy and Wayne agreed and the three men set to placing the stone bricks around the edge of the dig both to mark the area and because it gave them closure on the day's work to do so. Still, they were careful around the lip of opening, not entirely sure how stable it was and none too eager to find out how far down the water really lay. There would be time for satisfying curiosity the following day when they would set up a new rig for drawing water and hopefully wall the hole up enough to offer some rough protection from the elements.

"What'd you boys do to my mule," Bixby asked as the three well-diggers entered the front gate of the ranch. There was a smile on the man's face, but it didn't reach his eyes. Scott wondered if the old rancher was angry at what he perceived to be carelessness on the part of the workers or if it was something more.

"Sorry, boss," Wayne drawled. "Old Maybelle got spooked and took off on us. We was lucky not to be under her feet when she did, too."

"Yeah?" Bixby asked, skepticism clear in his voice. "Be that as it may, when you take an animal from my ranch, you take care of it, you hear? You don't let it run all over high hell and back because it gets a bug in its ear. You catch it, always, and you bring it home safe."

The ranch hand's abashed expression was sincere. "Won't let it happen again, boss."

Without replying, Bixby pulled the gloves from his back pocket and slipped them on over hands caked with something that looked like flour. "Get your gear stowed for the night and see to your horses. After that, I got some other work to keep you busy until Nan rings the supper bell."

Allen's limp was a great deal more pronounced as he led his pony into the coral than it had been that morning. The injured limb had obviously stiffened up during the ride back and was giving him trouble. A day of hard work out in the sun could suck the life out of any man, but the soldier tried to keep his back straight enough to hide his discomfort. He wasn't as successful as he had hoped.

"Don't you worry 'bout old Bixby," Wayne said as he began loosening the saddle of his mare. "He ain't paying you to do no extra chores around here." The ranch hand's cousin only grunted in reply, but the cowboy could see relief in the big man's eye.

Dinner passed uneventfully, much as it had before, though the simple fare the Indian woman brought out to them was plainer and less satisfying than the cowboy had come to expect. Nan almost stumbled as she made her way to and from the kitchen, and more than once Scott wondered if she might not be ill. The woman herself, as usual, did not speak to express her discomfort (or anything else for that matter) and generally avoided eye contact as she brought out the food. Scott wondered if the Indian woman even spoke any English, but he figured that she must have, given that she responded to Bixby's requests without any kind of hesitation or confusion. Colored women in those wild times did not tend to have the easiest of lives--Scott knew that first hand--so he could hardly blame Nan if she was less than social with a bunch of rough-spoken ranch hands who spent most of their days looking at cattle from behind.

The cowboy waited patiently to give his update on the day's progress, assuming that Bixby would want to talk about it at some point, but the old rancher remained stony silent during dinner and seemed to snub the men by leaving the table first and heading out the back of the house. If anyone but Scott thought the behavior was odd, however, they didn't bother to look up from their plates to say as much.

The three well-diggers succumbed to their exhaustion almost immediately that night, their weary bones fairly melting into their straw mattresses and their snores echoing through the hands' quarters before even a single lamp had been extinguished. There had been offers of whisky and cards by the other hands, but there were some siren songs too sweet not to follow and, that night, sleep was the sweetest of them all.

The cowboy stared down at the ring of bricks at his feet while the shadows of circling buzzards floated across them. In one hand he held one of the rectangular stones and he knew that its placement was key to unlocking the meaning of the image that lay spread out on the ground before him.

How long he had been standing there staring at the sandy colored objects he could not remember, but it was long enough for his skin to burn to an angry red and even begin to blister and peel where it stretched thinly across his knuckles. It didn't matter, though. Nothing mattered but finding the pattern in the mismatch of lines on the ground and discovering its hidden meaning.

The shadows of the buzzards grew and shrank as they rose and dipped above the cowboy and the earth shimmered with the brutal heat of high noon. When the stones began to move of their own accord, the cowboy thought it was simply an illusion stirred up by his fevered mind and he did not even bother to take a step away from them. He watched the bricks shift and slide into position, moved by some unseen force, until they were all together and he could almost see the picture of what they formed. There was a space in the middle, however, for the last brick—the one in his hand. The meaning of the pattern danced and flirted right at the edge of his understanding and somehow he knew that it would all be clear as soon as the last stone was in place.

Crouching, he stretched his arm forward towards the dark rectangular gap in the middle of the brick mosaic. The cowboy could see his hand trembling beneath the weight of the stone as his body became inexplicably sluggish. It was as if the midday sun had turned the air as hot and thick as a mud pot, keeping that final understanding at bay for as long as possible.

The feet slowly turned to inches until the brick was just above the last empty space. *I'm going to know*, the cowboy's mind exulted, *I'm going to see!* Just before he could lower the heavy stone, however, the shade beneath it took on a life of its own. It poured out of the gap in the ground like a fountain, rising up and wrapping coal black tendrils around his arm and melting through the sunburnt flesh as if it was so much red and brown lard.

The cowboy screamed as he saw his limb drop away from his body and hit the ground, the final stone still clutched tightly in its twitching fingers. The shadow continued to grow and pulsate until it towered over him, writhing like the shadow of some alien tree. Then, just in the middle of what would have been the trunk, the shadow opened into a gapping maw filled with an endless spiral of jagged white teeth...

None of the men in the cabin so much as stirred as the cowboy bolted upright in his cot, nearly tipping the shoddy bit of furniture clean over. His breath was ragged and his hair was plastered to his forehead with sweat as the terrifying final image of the dream slowly began to fade from his mind's eye. Scott's mouth felt as foul and dry as if he had been chewing on an old sock in his sleep and he knew that he wasn't going to get any more rest that night.

The cowboy walked barefoot across the rough wooden floor to pour himself a cup of water from a pitcher that sat under a big shard of broken mirror. It was something that one of the ranch hands had hung there for the purpose of shaving. The cowboy stared at his own dim reflection in the glass for only a brief moment before looking away. Though he knew it was foolish, he felt as if his own image was staring back at him with eyes that had fallen back into black pits. The dream, he realized, had shaken him up more than he had originally thought. It wasn't surprising, really, given the unsettling events down in the town well, Bixby's disturbing story, and countless hours toiling out in the sun. *Hell*, Scott though, *it would be stranger if I was feeling like my regular self tonight*.

The water pitcher turned out to be empty and the cowboy could not help but feel that he should have expected as much. Water was just never to be had when it was most wanted those days. Since he had already given up on the idea of getting any sleep that night, a solitary walk out to Bixby's well for a cool drink was not an entirely unpleasant prospect. Just thinking about taking a deep gulp straight from the bucket make the cowboy's throat fairly quake in anticipation, and he didn't even bother to put on his boots before slipping quietly out into the night.

The well, if the cowboy remembered correctly, was located behind the house. It was convenient for the Indian woman, no doubt, but it must have been a hassle for the other workers who had to carry water bucket-by-bucket to fill the horses' troughs and, now, the chicken's water dishes as well. Thankfully, the cattle were watered mostly by a nearby stream and the cowboy was glad not to be around during a time when they, too, needed to be watered by hand.

The three-quarter moon rested high in the cloudless sky, illuminating the well-worn path from the hands' quarters to the big house, and the world was as mysteriously quiet as only those small hours of the morning can be. The windows of the house stared out vacantly between their shutters and only a faintest wisp of smoke curled silently from the thick stone chimney that raised its stubby head into the night sky.

Had it not been for that uncanny stillness, the cowboy might have lost his life standing barefoot in the darkness, for just as he was about to turn the corner of the east side of the house, Scott heard a soft rustling along the ground. *Snake*, his mind called out, and the cowboy froze in place. The night air washed coolly over his skin, but the hard packed ground was still surprisingly warm beneath his bare feet, as if he were standing in a spot where a great animal had just risen from a long nap. Surely no snake could have caused that, a horse or steer perhaps, but the sound that he heard was far too faint and subtle to be anything as large and heavy as a horse climbing to its feet. Besides, there was no reason for any of the animals to be out at that time of night and even less reason for one of them to take a rest so close to the house.

The cowboy's thoughts were interrupted by the sound again and, not seeing any movement within his current field of vision, began to creep silently to the corner of the house. What he saw as he peered around the wooden corner post stunned him with the force of a physical blow.

The dark thing was more than a shadow, he realized, somehow darker and heavier than the natural shadows around it. It even seemed to shimmer slightly in the moonlight as it moved.

Whatever it was, the cowboy could not make out a discernible shape in dim lighting, though it was clear that the shadowy thing was larger than a man and did not move like any natural creature he had ever seen. The thing shifted rapidly away from the house and towards the well where it quickly slithered up the side and vanished from sight with no further sound than the slight *shoosh* noise that Scott heard.

The entire scene had played out in only the time it had taken the cowboy to take two or three breaths, yet it had felt like an eternity. Fear had frozen him in place and possibly prevented him from being noticed by whatever that thing was.

Once the spell was broken, the cowboy felt his knees give out and he slid slowly to the ground, the wall of the house supporting him from behind. The young wanderer ran his fingers through his hair and tried to come to grips with the episodes of insanity that had suddenly began to bleed into his otherwise unremarkable life and he wondered, not for the first time, if he could really trust what his eyes were telling him. If not for Bixby's story about his uncle, Jim, the cowboy might have already accepted as a fact that he had lost his mind somewhere between leaving the Prescott ranch and finding the pitiful dried up streets of Drum Hollow.

Maybe I need to be done out here, he considered. The cowboy loved the freedom of riding from job to job with nothing to tie him down and the brief but intense bonds formed between men who had faced hardship together, but was it worth knowing that tucked within the depths beneath the surrounding peaceful plains lay secrets so terrible his that mind rejected them as madness? That was a burden he would have traded anything he owned to be rid of. He wondered if there was any place Windkicker could carry him that would be far enough away to even begin to forget what he had learned.

Too afraid to make his way back through the darkness, the cowboy remained rooted to the ground until the first light of day slowly broke over the horizon and released him from the night's dark embrace. His body stiff and his throat still raw with thirst, Scott made his way back to the hands' quarters figuring that it was too early for anyone to have noticed his absence. If anyone did mark his early morning entry, the cowboy thought, he would simply say that he had gone out for a piss that took longer than expected. Ranch hands and cowpunchers had little time to themselves so it wasn't unheard of for them to take some time to amuse themselves within the confines of an outhouse if that was all the privacy they could expect to find on a given day.

As it turned out, Allen's were the only open eyes when the cowboy slipped quietly back into the building, but the soldier did not seem particularly interested in how any of the inhabitants of the bunkhouse spent their time and so he did not bother with so much as a greeting, let alone a barrage of unwanted questions. Shortly after, the rest of the men began to stir and make their morning toilet before another day of honest labor began.

Though he desperately wished to do so, the cowboy kept the previous night's events to himself and tried to behave as it if was any other day. Still, he would not drink the coffee that was offered to him at the breakfast table and advised the others likewise. The looks of incredulity they gave him at that simple suggestion cemented in his mind the wisdom of not trying to convince the ranch hands that he had seen some kind of monster climb down into their water supply a few hours earlier.

The cowboy thought that Bixby, at least, would want to know what he had seen, but the older man looked far more irritable than usual at breakfast that morning. His eyes were rimmed with red and he didn't speak a word that didn't come out as an angry bark. He said that he had heard coyotes howling in the east pasture the night before and that heads would roll if he found a downed stretch of fence and a dead calf.

It didn't help matters that breakfast consisted of nothing more than boiled eggs and leftover biscuits, brought out by the boss man himself no less. If old Nan had been under the weather last night, she must have been completely laid up that morning to let such pathetic fare pass for a morning meal at her table.

Substandard grub aside, the cowboy was struck but how much of a change the old man had undergone since their first meeting just a few days before. The rancher's face was drawn and his posture seemed almost hunched. Could having dredged up that terrible memory of his Uncle Jim have been enough to bring about such a change?

Come to think of it, those first couple of hours at the Bixby ranch were the only ones when the old rancher had reminded the cowboy fondly of his departed step-father.

After that, Bixby had rather quickly become less and less pleasant until he might have been any number of other bosses the cowboy had had the misfortune to work for. Just the way he had chewed out good-natured Wayne for letting Maybelle (an animal the hand clearly adored) come home alone showed not only a lack of compassion, but a lack of character in general. So which one was the real Edward Bixby?

Scott opened his mouth to ask the old rancher if he was feeling okay when Bixby stopped him with a withering stare. "You boys going to finish that well today?"

"Yes, sir. We reckon to do so." The cowboy noticed that the dining area had suddenly and completely vacated, leaving the two men alone.

"Good. Because, if you're not, that's too bad for you and for those damned fools in town. I need my men working here. *All* of them." The old rancher took a step closer. "You hear me, boy? I ain't sending Wayne out there to play in the dirt when there's coyotes and worse what need to be dealt with. And who the hell do you think is taking care of James's chickens now that I've their hungry beaks to stuff every day?"

The cowboy held up his hands defensively. "You been more than generous, Mr. Bixby. Ain't nobody can say different.

195

We're just about done out there as it is and I'm itching to move on myself."

"You see that you do," Bixby fairly snarled. "I would say that you have most certainly worn out your welcome here, boy" he added before turning away and storming into the hidden confines of Nan's kitchen.

Had the old man gone mad? Whatever had gotten under Bixby's skin, the old man seemed none too eager to talk about it and it wasn't really Scott's problem to begin with. If there was something creeping around behind the big house at night, well, the people of the ranch would just have to find out for themselves. No one but Bixby would believe the cowby's story and he was none too inclined to hear anything the drifter had to say that morning.

The best thing to do, as the cowboy saw it, was to finish his work and start making his way east. A man who knew his letters could make a life for himself just about anywhere if he talked to the right people. Though his heart told him that he was too young to tie himself to someone else's desk somewhere, the cowboy's brain was telling him that a smart horse and well-oiled gun were proving to be too little to count on if a man wanted to survive in an increasingly unknowable world.

That last thought reminded the cowboy that he hadn't tended to his weapon in a while. Riding the dusty trail was hard on a pistol and the last thing he wanted was for the damned thing to jam on him when he needed it most. For the last couple of days, he had been content to drape his gun belt over Windkicker's saddle horn while he engaged in the more intensively physical of the day's labor. After what he had seen the previous night, however, he wasn't going to spend another minute in the wild without his gun either in his belt or in his hand.

"You going to stand there all day, or were you expecting me to carry you out?"

Allen's voice startled the cowboy out of his thoughts. "No. Yeah. Sorry."

The soldier's broad shoulders fairly filled the doorframe. "Well, let's get to it. The way I figure, we oughta be done by noon today. I can't say as it hasn't been interesting working with you, cowboy, but my ma needs me and I need to feel my own bed beneath me at night. You follow?"

He did follow, and Scott felt an unexpected pang of sorrow as he was reminded of the home he no longer had to go back to. He let a sharp breath out of his nose to clear his head of the thought. It was not a fitting time to wax nostalgic and the cowboy well knew it. "I hear you," he replied. "Never let it be said that I would knowingly stand between a soldier and his favorite blanket."

Allen grinned fiercely. "Good man. Now move your ass."

Chapter Fourteen

Maybelle stood rooted in the center of the two dusty ruts that served as the road north of Drum Hollow. No amount of coaxing on Wayne's part (nor cursing on Allen's) could get the beast to budge. The animal's stubborn streak the ranch hand could handle, but the terror that was so clear in her eyes that morning was another story. Allen suggested that they just drag her until she decided that fighting wasn't worth the trouble, but not even his impressive frame could move a two-thousand pound mule that was bent on staying put.

The group had only made it about five minutes from the ranch before Maybelle decided to protest and so the three men headed back and unloaded her heavy cargo of mortar mix and other miscellaneous supplies from mule's back and into the wagon and hooked up the horses. Though there was an edginess about the other beasts as well, they were at least willing to be lead back to the worksite without a struggle.

"They don't like that hole we made," Wayne noted as the wagon pulled to a stop. "Might be best to not push them into getting too close or they might try to bolt and end up flipping the wagon all together."

The cowboy was the only man mounted on his own animal, but he fully agreed with the ranch hand's suggestion. Like the other two horses, Windkicker was tense in a way that Scott had never experienced before, and that sense of unease was catching. The cloth sacks of mortar were not so heavy nor the distance so far that they could not keep the animals at a comfortable distance from where the work was to be done, and so that seemed like the wisest course of action if the three men wanted to avoid any more violent attempts at escape.

Allen grumbled about not taking a bullet in the war so he could return home to do a goddam mule's job, but it was mostly for show. The truth of the matter was that the soldier was proud of having found the water and dug it up and he wanted to see the job finished right. As eager as he was to return home, he would not do so until he was satisfied that the legacy of his well was completed entirely to his liking.

Dark Rivers

The cowboy and Allen sent the rope and bucket down the hole while Wayne unloaded the rest of the supplies. The two men were not entirely sure how far down the water lay, having left in a bit of a hurry the day before, though they could hear it rushing clearly enough in the darkness below. The well would not be a practical source of water if the average woman or child could not haul a full bucket from its depths, however, and so they were relieved when they felt the current grab hold and fill the bucket after less than fifteen feet of rope had been let out.

The battered tin bucket came up with the same clean and surprisingly cold water they had found in the cavern, and they wasted no time in using it to mix up a batch of thick gray mortar. None of the men had much experience with masonry, so it was unlikely that they were going to create a perfectly symmetrical cylinder as might be found in a fairytale illustration, but their efforts would suffice and the entrance to the well would be protected, if not beautiful.

The circumference of the ring of bricks turned out to be wider than originally intended and the pile of plain stones the cowboy had gathered was quickly spent. Originally Allen and Scott had not wanted to use the other bricks, the ones with the markings, in hopes of solving the mystery of their cryptic design, but it was clear that they would need to if they wanted to finish their work as quickly as possible--and they most certainly did.

Though there had already been a pervading sense of general unease among the workers that morning, a sudden shudder ran through the cowboy as he approached the clearing where the three men had tried to put the stones together like clunky puzzle pieces. His hand dropped unconsciously to the handle of his six-shooter for a moment and its familiar smoothness was a comfort, though he could not say just why.

"Seems like a waste to mix all these rocks up just to make a well," Wayne noted as he shoved three of the heavy bricks under his left arm. "Guess we'll never get to see what kind of picture they made."

"Too bad," Allen agreed, and he did seem to genuinely regret putting the stones to such a mundane use.

The cowboy remained silent on the issue. He was more than happy to have the damned things off the ground and put to some use other than keeping him awake at night. Once the bricks were wrapped neatly around the entrance to the well, Scott hoped in the far reaches of his mind, they would no longer have the power to evoke the image from his nightmare.

The work continued without further delay until the ring of stones rose in a relatively even three foot protective wall around the opening in the ground. It was just the right height, Wayne noted, for a man to trip over, but they all agreed that a fool who was dumb enough to fall into their new well was a fool that would not be sorely missed. Still, they had brought the old lumber along to make a lid to keep any animals, debris, or fools from dropping down and spoiling the clean water. The underground river might have been rushing at that moment, but there was no telling when it might dry up enough that unwanted rubbish would just sit at the bottom and sour the water instead of being washed away by it.

While Allen and his cousin argued about the best way to nail the boards together, the cowboy stood staring down into the murky depths the represented all of their hard labor. The air that rose up was damp and cool, but there was a slight tang as it entered his nostrils. *Minerals*, he guessed, though it was not the peasant earthy smell he associated from particularly hard water.

It was while he was pondering that thought that Scott saw something on the inside wall of the well that made his knees go weak in a fashion not unlike they had the night before. Consciously or unconsciously, the three men had placed the bricks so that all of the engraved lines faced the inside of the well. Although they did not come together as perfectly as they had on the ground, the cowboy saw that they formed a new ring of geometric shapes that linked to each other in a disturbing pattern. The more he stared at it, becoming almost hypnotized as the lines slid and shifted in his mind's eye, the less possible it was to look away.

Images began to form in his head of man-shaped shadows toiling under the desert sun. He saw them building what appeared to be an altar of yellow stones and calling to the sky in hopes of some unknowable answer. And then he heard it— the answer the man-shadows were waiting for—and its keening cry blasted into the cowboy's mind like a cloud of locusts. Quickly, the image began to shift and vibrate until he brought his hands up to his hears to block out the noise. But something terrible was coming, the cowboy knew that the same way he somehow knew that the carvings on the stones were guiding it towards him, and it was coming fast.

Scott's head began to swim as the vision filled it and just when he was about to cry out for it to stop, it ended as abruptly as it had started. The cowboy quickly turned his face away from the stones and emptied the contents of his stomach onto the ground in a burning gray stream of pulverized eggs and floury mush.

Finally, his knees did go out on him again and, with no wall to catch him, Scott crashed into the ground. His breakfast flowed by just inches from his fingers, but he did not notice. Instead, the cowboy just sat staring at the blankly at the smooth side of the stones while his head throbbed and his belly continued to churn.

"What in the Sam Hill," Allen said and rushed over to his fallen comrade, the extra haste combined with the worsening stiffness in his leg turned his usual limp into a full on lurch.

The cowboy wiped his mouth across the back of his wrist as the big man crouched beside him. "The stones," he croaked out of his bile-caked throat. "The pattern."

Allen peered briefly into the well but did not see what Scott had noticed and quickly turned back to him. "What kind of nonsense is this? I thought you got bit by a snake!" There was a mix of anger and relief in the soldier's words. "Now you're telling me that our shitty masonry skills are enough to make you puke?"

"I see it," Wayne said, but he was wise enough to turn away as soon as he felt the first twinge of nausea. "There's something ain't right about them. I see it," he repeated.

This time Allen got back to his feet and looked at the inside of the well. At first, all he saw was the darkness below and the even line of jutting stone that Maybelle had broken off the day before. But then he saw it, too. He saw how the lines and carvings of the bricks had unknowingly been placed together to make a pattern that seemed to shift and distort in nauseating waves no matter the angle it was approached from. "Impossible," the soldier grumbled, knowing that it was unthinkable that the stones could have been placed that way purely by accident. He gritted his teeth as the alien quality of the design pushed and prodded at his mind until he, too, relented and turned away.

"We can't just leave it like that," the cowboy choked out as he pushed himself up to his knees. "We can't."

"If you're thinking we's gonna tear down them stones after all our work," Wayne complained, "you got another think coming.

Ain't nobody going to notice something on the *inside* of a well anyway."

"You did," Scott noted.

Allen seemed to agree. "If there was ever a stupid thought that entered your mind and didn't exit your mouth," he chided his cousin, "I think you might just explode from the pressure of keeping it in."

"We don't need to tear down the wall," the cowboy explained, finally back on his feet but looking none too steady. "We'll just paint over the pattern with mortar. If you can't see it, then it can't get into your head."

Neither of the other men saw any flaw in the cowboy's logic, but Allen decided that the three of them should take turns applying the gray paste to the offensive design. None of them could stand to look at it long enough to complete the job on their own, and it made them all feel a little less foolish for wanting to hide the offending pattern if everyone was part of the effort. It was only a few extra minutes work, after all was said and done, and the brick structure actually looked a little sturdier for their efforts.

Once the task was finished, the cowboy began to pack up the equipment while Allen and Wayne put the finishing touches on the wooden cover. The uncharacteristically overcast sky didn't seem to offer much promise of rain, but it had made the morning's work more comfortable and it had probably gone much more quickly for that. Still, the cowboy hadn't had anything to drink since the night before and the sound of the rushing water called to his parched throat.

"Let me fill up my canteen before you put that thing on," Scott requested. It took him less than a minute to grab it from his saddle and pick up the rope and bucket.

"Now hold on there," Allen said. "We're set on fixing that rope to the lid so that it don't drop in." He pointed a thick finger at a knothole in the center of the middle board. "We're going to thread the rope up through there and knot it off."

"Like an anchor," Wayne said in his sleepy drawl, "only in reverse."

Allen frowned, but did not deign to reply to his cousin's observation. "Anyway, you might as well be the first one to test it out. But keep a hold of it at first, just in case it don't hold."

The cowboy thought it was a good design, though he wasn't sure how old Bixby would feel about his bucket being left behind. The veteran rancher the cowboy had met a few days earlier might have put up a mock fuss at the loss, Scott figured, but the one he had sat across at breakfast that morning was libel to spit blood when he heard that some bit of his property, no matter how trivial, had been intentionally left out for strangers to use. It was just one more observation that convinced the cowboy that the sooner he was on his way from the ranch, its unstable owner, and whatever the hell was turning the world so crazy, the better.

The bucket dropped down into the well and hit the surface of the water with a satisfying smack. The current was strong enough that it jerked the rope out of the cowboy's hand and he was grateful that it was indeed fastened securely to the lid leaning next to the brick enclosure. Allen grunted his approval when he saw that his design had proven to be sound.

Hand-over-hand, the cowboy pulled the bucket up and smiled as the cool clear liquid neared his face. He was tempted to plunge his head right in and take a deep drink when the notion struck him that Allen should have the privilege of taking the first swallow from the finished well. It was, after all, the soldier's skill and knowledge that had led them to the water to begin with. It had also been the larger man's powerful arms that had moved more than his fair share of earth during the initial dig.

Without a word, the cowboy held the bucket in front of him and passed it to the soldier. "After you," he said with a satisfied grin on his face. "You earned this."

"Don't mind if I do," Allen said, grasping the bucket in his meaty hands and hauling the rim of the tin container up to his lips. At first the big man drank normally, but soon he was dumping the water faster than he could swallow until it was running down his beard and onto his chest. Finally, after he had evidently drunk his fill, he poured the rest of the contents over his head and hooted loudly. "Woo-wee! If that don't wake you up in the morning!"

Wayne wandered over and clapped his cousin on the back appreciatively and took the bucket into his own long fingers. "I wouldn't mind trying that myself!"

The cowboy, having watched the refreshing-looking display, was fairly choked with thirst. But he figured he could wait a few more minutes. It turned out, however, that Wayne was willing to wait his turn. "After you, of course," the lanky man explained as he passed the bucket over.

Relieved, Scott wasted no time in hauling up another bucket, his biceps burning from the effort. Just as he was about to sooth his parched lips, however, he felt the bucket jerk violently from his hands and crash to the ground where the equally parched earth soaked up the spilled contents almost on contact.

"No," Allen groaned as he clutched painfully at his belly with one hand and supported himself on the cowboy's shoulder with the other. Scott did his best to hold the big man up but after a few moments it was all he could do to lower him slowly to the ground.

"Allen!" Wayne dropped down to his cousin's side. The ranch hand had never seen the soldier react so violently to anything he had eaten or drank in the past. In fact, Allen had often bragged of having a cast iron stomach and liver and how he had only wished he'd had a knee to match.

Drops of water beaded across the big man's face as he eyes began to roll back behind fluttering eyelids. His mouth hung slack and his tongue seemed to purple and swell until Allen's breath slowed to a thin wheeze. The soldier's skin, despite the heat, became cool and clammy to the touch and it was clear that he was slipping into unconsciousness.

"Go get a doctor," the cowboy yelled, grabbing Wayne's elbow and jerking him away from the man on the ground. "Take my horse and ride like hell."

"Ain't no doctor," Wayne said numbly, shock plain on his face.

"Then get the barber," the cowboy said. When the lanky man didn't respond, Scott grabbed his chin and forced him to make eye contact. "Are you listening to me, partner? You need to go *now*."

The ranch hand seemed to grasp what was being said and he nodded once before running back and untying Windkicker from the side of the wagon. The gentle horse was startled when the Wayne climbed into the saddle, but he didn't hesitate to live up to his name after he felt the familiar snap of the reins.

It only took a few seconds for man and horse to become a distant puff of dust and Scott was grateful that they were as close to town as they were. There was no telling what could be done for Allen but whatever it was, it needed to be done right quick. The trickle of blood that oozed from the big man's nose was a clear warning that whatever was wrong with him was only getting worse.

The cowboy placed his hand on Allen's chest and felt that the soldier's heart was beating with force, but entirely too quickly. Scott wanted to say something, to thank the big man for knocking the bucket away when he did, but the words just didn't come. Instead he loosened Allen's collar and mopped the moisture from his face with his own handkerchief.

Though it felt like an eternity while the cowboy waited, it wasn't more than ten minutes before Wayne returned with a tall, silver-bearded man riding a sleepy-looking paint. The cowboy recognized him from town and thought his name might be Craig or Greg or some such thing. The barber hopped from his mount with a small black bag in hand and, skipping all polite introductions, laid his head against Allen's chest.

"How long has he been like this?" the gray haired man asked, pulling a pair of small spectacles from his shirt pocket and balancing them on the end of his nose.

"I'm not sure," the cowboy admitted. "Maybe ten minutes or so. He just dropped over after drinking from that well."

The barber frowned. "Don't you fools know the water ain't no good in these parts?" Then the older man realized who he was talking to. "Hell, if anybody knows it, it should be you."

"We checked it," Wayne argued. "If this water ain't good now, it sure as hell was good yesterday."

"No," the cowboy said as the horror of the situation dawned on him. "The water at the cavern was good, but we don't know that it didn't go sour somewhere after that."

"But you said the water east of town was good. Even old Bixby agreed to as much," the ranch hand argued.

The tall man interrupted. "I ain't interested in who thought what and when, but it's clear as the sun is hot that the water ain't no good now and Allen here is plenty proof of that."

The other two men looked on helplessly while the barber checked the big man's eyes and looked down in his throat with a tiny mirror on the end of a silver rod. After he listened to Allen's heart one more time, he stood up and brushed off the dusty knees of his long dark pant legs.

"His heartbeat is strong and his airway is open so he'll live," the tall man declared. "Though I can't say for how long. I'm sorry to tell you that there ain't nothing more I can do for him. If he had a busted leg or a rotten tooth, I'd be first in line to patch him up, but this is beyond my ken."

"His mama is gonna kill me," Wayne lamented.

"You just hush up, boy," the barber scolded, "and keep that cry-baby nonsense to yourself. Let's try to load him up in that wagon of yours and at least get him back to his own bed."

It was no small task getting the big man off the ground, but the three of them together eventually managed it. There was a moment when the cowboy thought that Allen might be regaining consciousness, but the lolling head and weak groans only signified that the big man was suffering. *That could have been me,* the cowboy thought, and a guilty little part of him half-wished that it was.

The thin but merciful cover of clouds had evaporated and the hot morning air had become a blast furnace by the time Allen was resting in his mother's double-wide bed. Wayne insisted that his cousin would have wanted to be in his own room, but there was just no way they were going to get his considerable bulk up to the second floor. Already, Craig, Wayne, and the cowboy were soaked through with sweat and they drank thirstily from the pump outside Jesse's modest home, once they were satisfied that Allen was as comfortable as they could make him.

None of them felt completely at ease drinking from the water, even that far away from the two sour wells, but thirst was a brutal master and would not let fear keep the men from filling their bellies. Once satisfied, they found their entry back into the house blocked by Jesse and what looked to be a military issue rifle clutched desperately in two shaky hands.

"Now what's this about?" Craig asked. "It ain't gonna hurt to let me go in and check on him one more time."

"Ain't going to help, neither," the woman replied fiercely. "None of that butcher's work you did in the war is going help my boy now, and he ain't in need of a trim neither." Her voice had begun to tremble slightly. "He's handsome just as he is."

"I'm awful sorry, Auntie, and I—" Wayne started. All it took was a look from his aunt and he backed meekly away.

The woman was done with words, no mistake about that, and all three of the men decided to make a hasty retreat before she started speaking with bullets instead fierce looks. It was true that none of them even knew what was wrong with Allen, let alone the knowledge to help him, and Jesse was bent on keeping her son safe the only way she could at that moment.

"He's gonna be alright, ain't he?" Wayne asked pleadingly as the barber slipped a booted foot into the stirrup, but all Craig could do was shrug in response.

"If anybody could survive the sour water," the barber replied, "it'd be that old warhorse. If one of you two beanpoles had drank half as much as Allen, I reckon I'd be measuring you for a pine box by now. Helluva way to go that would be, eh?" With that, he pulled himself into the saddle and started slowly back to town.

Scott drew the brim of his hat a little farther over his eyes to block out the glare of the sun. "Come on, hoss," he said to Wayne whose naturally long face had manage to appear even longer. "Let's head out. Ain't nothing more we can do here."

The words came out of his mouth easily enough, but the cowboy's heart was heavy as they made their way back through town. Albert scowled at him from the porch of his saloon as they passed and Scott wondered if word of the new well had started to spread already. Given how little settlements like Drum Hollow worked, he didn't doubt it. If the crotchety old barkeep continued to hold some kind of grudge against him, well then, the cowboy felt that he had finally earned it.

Chapter Fifteen

"Means little and less to me," Bixby said after Wayne explained what had happened. "I thought digging a hole to water those simps and ingrates in Drum Hollow was about as big a waste of time as a man could think up in a day. I don't know who was the bigger fool—me for playing along with that cowboy's game or your cousin for drinking out of a sour well." The old man's voice was as hard and cruel as the cowboy had recently come to expect, but his eyes just looked tired.

Wayne's spirit, not the boldest to begin with, was overwhelmed with hurt and guilt over his cousin's affliction and could only bring himself to shy away from the old rancher's harsh words. "I'm going to join the boys and get some work done," was all he could manage to mutter before slinking off like a kicked dog.

The cowboy was dangerously close to striking the rancher, old man or not, for the way he had just treated perhaps the gentlest man to ever rope a calf. Wayne might not have been the brightest candle in the church, but he was far more honest and loyal than Bixby deserved. Scott kept his anger in check, however. He was done with the well and, although he felt bad about Allen, there was nothing left for him to do but hit the trail and find a new life wherever the world would have him.

"I guess I'm done here then," the cowboy stated, sniffing once and frowning at the man before him. "I'm just gonna pick up my kit from the bunkhouse and be on my way."

"Just like that," Bixby said in a mocking tone just as the cowboy turned away from him.

"Just like what?" Scott demanded, his general good nature all but worn away.

"You're going to ride off without so much as a thank you and a handshake." The old rancher turned and spat out a wad of dark brown phlegm, a few drops of which beaded in his beard. "I guess I shouldn't have expected no more from some half-breed drifter come begging at my door."

The cowboy's mounting anger shifted to confusion. Bixby was clearly baiting him, but just what was the old man's game? "I'm thankful for what you did for Ezra and his girl, if that's what you mean."

Bixby snorted and spat again, this time running his mouth across the back of his sleeve. It left a streak so dark that the cowboy wondered if what he had original thought was chaw juice might not be blood. "I'm talking about me taking you in, boy! I broke bread with you at my table and shared my whisky. And how do you replay me?"

The cowboy just stood and waited for the old man to continue. As far as Scott knew, he hadn't done anything to bring inspire so much ire in Bixby. If he had, he sure as hell wanted to know what it was.

Since the cowboy wasn't forth coming with an apology, the rancher continued after a few uncomfortable seconds. "You *repay* me by running around digging holes in the ground, letting my animals run wild, and sticking your damned nose where it don't belong."

"Look, Mr. Bixby," the cowboy said, slipping his thumbs into the pockets of his trousers. "You knew full well why we were out there digging that well and you gave us your blessing. I didn't take nothing that wasn't offered to me and that includes the use of your mule. As for not minding my own business, I didn't never ask you anything as you didn't offer up yourself. I don't make it a habit of collecting other people's secrets and I as sure as shit didn't plan on starting with you."

Then a thought dawned on him. For a moment the cowboy thought he understood what this was all about—old Bixby's sudden change in attitude, the disapproval of the well, all of it. The old man was ashamed. He had shared a memory from his past so painful that it had moved him to tears in front of a near stranger. After time to reflect, the old rancher probably regretted making himself appear so weak and vulnerable and his way of covering for it was to try to come across as harsh and no-nonsense after the fact. Never mind that he was only making an ass of himself in the process. It wouldn't be the first time a man's pride led him to foolishness.

"What I'm talking about," Bixby clarified, "is you sneaking around my place in the middle of the night. What were you looking for under Nan's window, boy?"

That genuinely took the cowboy by surprise and he felt himself flush with embarrassment. There had been no lights on the house the night before and he hadn't heard so much as the rustling of a bed sheet as he had sat waiting for the dawn.

The old rancher grinned cruelly. "Bet you didn't think I knew that, eh boy? Them Injuns don't sleep like other folks and they know when trouble's coming. Wake up just like deer when the scent of a wolf tells them an enemy is nearby. Yes, they do. You some kind of wolf then, cowboy? Maybe hoping to catch a glimpse of old Nan diddling her wrinkled-up body in the wee hours while you follow suit?"

"What?" Scott was at a loss for words. "It weren't nothing like that!" The cowboy's head buzzed with frustration and he felt as off balance as a newborn foal. One second he was thinking Bixby was just putting on airs and the next minute he was fending off accusations of being a peeping tom.

"What *was* it like then, cowboy? Why don't you teach me something with all of them laundry woman smarts your mama blessed you with." Bixby's arms were crossed in front of his chest and the expression on his face made clear that he wasn't going to believe anything the younger man said regardless of how plausible.

"I just went to get a drink is all." Scott felt the need to defend himself, so he tried explaining regardless of how futile the effort might have been. "That's when I heard something moving by the house. I saw some big shadow or something by your well and, given what I've seen and heard these past few days, I got spooked. I would think that you of all people could understand something like that."

Bixby squinted at the cowboy for a moment. "That your story?"

"It's the truth," the cowboy said. Now that his initial embarrassment was fading, he felt his anger beginning to bubble up again.

"Well, let's just say that I believe you then." Bixby's tone of voice shifted from accusatory to almost philosophical. "I'm not saying as there was anything worth you getting all worked up over, but let's just imagine that, for the sake of argument, you really were just hiding out by the house because you was scared. Even if that is true, where does that leave old Nan?"

"What do you mean?"

"What I mean," the old rancher said, thrusting an accusing finger at the cowboy, "is that you put a scare into her, that's what. Some strange man sitting outside her window all night? Shoot! You're lucky I didn't catch you out there myself or you'd have gone to bed tonight with a few extra holes in your backside."

"Okay," the cowboy admitted. "I see what you mean. If you want me to say sorry to the woman before I leave, I guess that's fair." His shifting tide of emotion moved away from anger and embarrassment and settled on shame and acquiescence. If all it took was an apology to clear the air and get himself away from the ranch with more understanding and fewer hurt feeling, Scott was willing to eat a little crow. "I didn't mean to put no scare in her. That's the honest truth."

Bixby seemed to relax at that. "Honest, eh? I guess I can't ask for no more than an honest man then. Nan's out back right now scrubbing down some laundry and I bet it would do her old heart good to hear you tell her what you done just told me."

Scott pinched the bridge of his nose and let out a sigh. "Alright. I'll make my peace with your Indian woman and we part ways like gentlemen. Agreed?"

The older man nodded. "Just as you say, boy. Just as you say."

Old Nan was sitting on a low bench crouched over a tub filled with filmy water. The stench of lye was almost overpowering, but the Indian woman didn't seem to mind. Neither did it seem to bother her that the caustic solution appeared to be eating angry holes in the shirt she was scrubbing as well burning into the leathery flesh of her hands. If it caused her any discomfort, the almost comically large sunbonnet that surrounded her face hid any sign of it. The old woman didn't bother to greet or otherwise acknowledge the two men as they approached to interrupt her work.

"Nan, this boy has something to tell you."

The woman looked up and the cowboy was amazed by the deep and complex web of wrinkles that covered Nan's face. While he had originally thought her to be of an age with Bixby, she now looked like she could have passed for twenty or maybe thirty years his senior. Even her eyelids seemed to sit like empty saddlebags over her cheeks, as if they had grown too weary over time to maintain their proper position.

Having never heard the Indian woman speak, the cowboy didn't wait for further invitation. "Ma'am," he began. Suddenly aware of the awkwardness of what he was about to say, Scott took his hat off and held it in front of him before continuing. "I have come to understand that you saw me sitting by the house last night."

Nan's expression did not change. It did not, in fact, appear as if there was enough elasticity in her face to do more than remain hanging loosely from her skull. It unnerved the already anxious cowboy even to look at her, so he shifted his eyes to the rough-hewn wooden post her stool rested against.

"I just want you to know that I weren't looking in no windows—not a one. If you thought that maybe I was trying to infringe upon your privacy or take advantage of your trusting nature, I want to assure you that it was not the case." He paused to clear his throat. "I loved my own mamma dearly and I would not dishonor her memory by being so dastardly as to disrespect the privacy of a fine woman such as yourself."

Since the Indian woman still did not respond in any way beyond her vacant stare, the cowboy wondered if maybe she hadn't understood him. He had, after all, thrown in a few two-dollar words into his apology to give it more weight, but perhaps that attempt had backfired on him. He looked to Bixby for a hint of what to do, but the old man simply rolled his finger forward in an impatient gesture for Scott to continue.

Shifting uncomfortably and squeezing at the brim of his hat, the cowboy struggled for more words. "And I, uh—I want you to know that I appreciate you having me in your home. You make some fine biscuits and I ain't never seen a house so clean on a ranch before. You ought to be right proud." He stopped there, clearly at a loss as to what more he could possibly add.

"Tell her why you were by her window!" Bixby snapped, causing the cowboy to flinch in surprise.

Scott continued, more cautiously than before, given that he was not entirely sure how much he wanted to reveal. "Well, about that. You see, I had a bad experience with the town well a few days ago and that's left me a little jumpy. When I went out to get some water last night, I thought I saw something behind your house and it stirred up them feelings again and really rattled me. I was so shook up, in fact," the cowboy looked to Bixby one more time and then back to the stoic leather mask that passed for the woman's face, "that I just froze up and sat under your window until daylight came. I left just as fast as I could after that—I swear to you—and I didn't see nothing inappropriate. In fact, I didn't even know that it was your window I was sitting under."

The cowboy put his hat back on as he considered the apology to be about as finished as it was going to get. "So no hard feelings, Ma'am. I wish you a fine day and many more to follow."

Just as he was turning to leave the Indian woman's hand shot out from the water in an aromatic arc of filmy liquid and latched on to the bottom of the cowboy's

227

vest. Scott cried out in surprise and even a little disgust. Nan stared up at him as if she was waiting for something more, but, still, she said nothing.

"I'd wager she wants to know just what it is you think you saw behind the house last night," Bixby explained. "I don't think she's liable to accept your apology until you make that part clear."

By that point, the cowboy didn't much care what the woman accepted, but he decided he'd come far enough with the apology that he could play along and humor Nan for a few more minutes. He really had meant what he had said about his mother and the importance of respecting women and Scott figured that was particularly true for a woman like Nan, who likely did not receive much from the rough spoken men in Bixby's employ.

"It weren't much, you see, just a shadow." The cowboy closed his eyes and tried to think back to the night before. It was something that he had wanted to just forget about but, perhaps, he would feel better for telling the old woman. Maybe he could leave the memory, and everything that had followed it, behind a little easier. "I thought I heard it—heard *something*— moving through the grass by the side of the house. It could have been a trick of my mind, but at the time it seemed that some kind shadowy thing was moving around. I watched it make its way across your yard and right up into your well."

The cowboy let out a nervous bark of laughter. "Hell! I was so shook up by it that I didn't even drink the coffee this morning. You know, because it was made from the well water." He could feel his hands shaking as he relived the memory and Scott promptly decided that he did not feel the least bit better for having spoken about the previous night's events.

"Now was that so hard?" Bixby asked, pulling gently at Nan's fingers where they still clutched at the cowboy's vest. "I think you told her just what she wanted to hear. Ain't that right, old girl?"

The woman's only reply was to push herself to her feet and shuffle silently into the house. The cowboy watched dejectedly as she went and worried that his misunderstood actions had offended Nan more deeply than he had even considered possible. Wayne had said something about her having been ostracized by her tribe for not being able to have babies, so maybe she had become so ashamed of her body that even the thought of some strange man peeping at her upset her on a more meaningful level than other women. It was either that, or she thought that the cowboy was a damned fool for being too afraid of shadows to return to his own bed at night.

"I'm sorry to have troubled her like I did," Scott said as he began to back away from the back porch. His expression was troubled and his voice sincerely apologetic. "I think it's just best if I be on my way and you won't never have no trouble from me again."

Bixby's expression had lost much of its hard edge and he seemed surprisingly at ease. "Nonsense. Why, I think old Nan is feeling a good deal better because of your honest and heartfelt admission." The old rancher smiled thinly. "It's hard to tell with Injun women, though. Don't take it too hard that she didn't clasp you to her bosom or nothing."

"I certainly hope she feels as better about it as you say," the cowboy replied, though he did not believe anything of the sort. Still, Windkicker was waiting and the guilt of offending the old woman was just one more thing that Scott planned on leaving behind. Eventually the madness of the past few days would fade into obscurity and the cowboy would hopefully chalk it up to a young mind fevered by thirst and the desert sun.

Pinching the brim of his hat by way of bidding farewell, Scott turned his back on the rancher and his face towards the future. With his mind so set on things to come, it was no surprise that he did not spare a thought to the sound of the washboard being drawn out of the lye-laden tub. The cowboy did not see as the old man approached. Bixby, with a determined strength and speed that belied his age, brought the side of the wooden implement crashing down against the back of Scott's skull. He did see the stars, however. They exploded in front of him just before his body dropped bonelessly to the ground.

Chapter Sixteen

Although the world was awash with a chaos of bright flashes mixed with purple blotches, the cowboy managed to avoid falling into unconsciousness. He was vaguely aware of Bixby dragging him hurriedly onto the porch before another smaller, but remarkably stronger, pair of hands seized him and jerked him into the house as if he were no more than a neck-wrung chicken. Scott was thrown unceremoniously into a rickety wooden chair next to a flower-caked table with a small pile of withered onions resting in the middle.

Scott could hear Bixby's heated voice for a while and it sounded as if the old man were arguing with himself, since no other voice answered during the measured pauses in his speech. It did not seem to matter much, given that the befuddled young man could not make sense of the words nor fully focus his eyes for several minutes. Before too much time had passed, however, the fog of his mind began to clear and was replaced by the sensation of an ice pick being driven squarely into the back of his head.

The cowboy's hat hung from his neck by a thin leather thong and when he reached back to touch underneath it, he nearly screamed from the fresh lance of agony that seemed to reach all the way to the soles of his feet. He clenched his teeth to hold the sound back, but when he saw that his fingers were now sticky with blood, a low moan escaped from his throat.

Bixby's voice, little more than a steady drone coming from across the room, suddenly stopped. The cowboy looked up and the two men's eyes met just as the rancher began to move towards his captive. It was a reflex, honed during endless hours in the saddle with nothing better to fill the time, that made all the difference just then.

There was no conscious decision to draw his weapon, but a split second after seeing the old rancher's face, the cowboy discovered it in his hand nonetheless.

The end of the barrel quivered from the effort of holding it in place until Scott rested his elbow on the table to steady it. Although at that moment the cowboy doubted he could manage to pull back the hammer without using both hands, the pearl handle of the six-shooter put a little steel back into his spine and, judging by Bixby's sudden decision to stop his momentum in mid-lunge, took a little out of his assailant's, too.

A shadow shifted behind the rancher and, for a moment, the cowboy was afraid that one of the hands had returned early. Though Scott got along well enough with Bixby's men, there was no doubt in his mind that they would side with the man who filled their pockets and bellies before some mongrel stranger holding an old man at gunpoint in his own home. When there was no sound of footsteps or other signs that anyone else had entered the house after a few seconds, however, the cowboy let out a breath that he hadn't even realized he was holding.

"I didn't hit you as hard as I thought," was all that the old man had to say as he stared at the weapon and began to back away through the narrow kitchen. When the cowboy did not reply, Bixby continued. "I could have cracked your skull clean open, you know, if'n I wanted to. But that just wouldn't do, now would it?"

"Why is that?" the cowboy asked in an icy voice.

"What's the point in catching a strong young buck like yourself," the rancher almost snarled, "just to have him bleed to death in my own damn kitchen?"

The situation did not make any kind of sense that the cowboy could conceive of, but he knew without even trying that it would still be a couple of minutes before he would be able to get to his feet. Every time he so much as shifted his body, his head swam and it was as much as he could manage not to throw up in his own lap. If he showed any such weakness at that moment, Bixby would be on him like the cunning old wolf he had proven himself to be. The cowboy might have been playing a charade at the moment, but it was still better for him to try to buy a little time than to let his true condition show.

"So why don't you just lay it all out for me, old son," the cowboy said. "You sure ain't the man I broke bread with a few days ago—the one who let a little girl sleep by his fire and lent his own hired hand to dig a well for people he didn't owe nothing to."

Bixby slid down to the ground, his back resting against the side of an old wooden pantry. "That I ain't, boy. That I surely ain't."

The rancher might have looked resigned to being held helplessly at gunpoint, slumped against cupboard as he was, but Scott did not trust the man any farther than he could throw him with a broken arm. The injured man never let his eyes drift from Bixby who, for all he knew, might have a rifle stashed just behind the pantry he was resting against. "So why all this then?" The cowboy asked. "If you're in some kind of trouble, you could have just asked for my help. You might not know me well, but surely you must know me enough to figure that I'd do what I could for you."

The rancher barked out a short pained laugh. "That's rich, cowboy. That's just too rich, being that you're the one that brought this trouble down on me in the first place," the old man's eyes blazed with fury, "and seen fit to just ride away from all of it, too. Don't you sit there and lie to my face and say that you care what happens to me, or to the good men who work for me neither."

"I don't know what you're talking about," Scott answered truthfully.

"Don't you?" Bixby snorted. "A book-learned man like yourself ain't figured it out yet?"

The cowboy could feel a burn building in his arm from holding the weapon up and slowly lowered it until his hand rested on the edge of the table. "Educate me."

"That thing you shot down in the well, boy—you think you killed it?"

The cowboy nodded. "I reckon so. I don't know that the shooting did much harm, but the fire and the roof caving in like it did must have finished it off."

"Yeah," Bixby explained, "it did. But not right away. You see, that thing laid there under them rocks screaming out its rage and agony for quite some time. It wasn't something that you or I would hear, at least not with our ears, but what would you guess about others like it?"

"What others?" The cowboy didn't like where this was heading.

"Don't play stupid, boy!" Spittle flew from the old man's lips before his voice dropped to an almost nervous whisper. "You *know* there are others. You sat right there in that next room while I told you about Jim."

"But that don't mean—"

Bixby cut him off. "It does too mean that. You can try to lie to yourself, boy, but not to me. That thing you saw in the well ain't the same one as I saw in Jim's creek."

"How do you know that?" the cowboy demanded.

"Because the thing I saw all them years ago came back. It came back because it heard the call of one of its kind—the one that called out because *you* had to play the hero by going down in that damned well!" The old man's voice rose again. "Why the hell couldn't you have just left well enough

237

alone and kept on riding straight through that cursed town?"

"Then none of this would have happened," the cowboy finished for him.

"That's right," the rancher agreed. "I could have forgotten about what happened to Uncle Jim, the people of Drum Hollow would have gotten thirsty enough and moved on, and—" He stopped abruptly, his ire plain on his face.

"And what?"

"And a sweet old Injun woman and a down-on-his-luck widower and his girl would still have a place in this world, that's what." Bixby's mouth twitched as he wrestled with his anger towards the cowboy and the guilt of his sudden admission.

The cowboy, however, felt no such conflicting emotions. He immediately pushed himself to his feet and, feeling his legs turn to jelly, just as quickly dropped back down with an angry exhalation. He wanted nothing more than to stride across the room, pull the old man up by his shirt collar, and beat the rest of the truth out of him.

Instead, Scott took a deep, calming breath and pulled the hammer of his pistol back with a surprisingly steady thumb. "I think you'd better tell me the rest of this story, old man, while I still have the patience to listen to it."

A low chuckle told the cowboy that the rancher was not intimidated by the weapon. "Shoot me if you want to," he invited. "It might be better than I deserve. But then you'd better just turn that barrel back at your own face to make things even."

The cowboy's gaze remained stony. "I'm listening."

Bixby seemed relieved at the chance to pour his guts out and the rest of the story came without hesitation.

The cowboy and Wayne had been busy filling buckets with life-giving water from the cavern when the chicken farmer and his daughter approached the ranch with their feathery offering bouncing in tow. Having neither horse nor wagon to move the animals, Ezra had managed to trade his meager homestead for a pallet mounted on four stubby wheels and a pair of half-worn boots, which he was already wearing in place of his previous tattered footwear. It wasn't much of a trade, but the fleeing man had originally planned to take his daughter and just walk away from it all and leave its fate to whomever decided it was worth the trouble of tending to. To Ezra, getting *anything* in trade was a bargain.

The chickens clucked quietly from behind the thin wooden bars of their makeshift cages. They weren't used to traveling and didn't much care for the experience. Still, it had been no small feat to pull them all the way from town through the summer heat and Ezra was mighty grateful to have made it to the ranch without dropping beneath the oppressive weight of the late morning sun.

Bixby was already waiting by the ranch's sun-faded gate when the chicken farmer approached and directed him where to put the chickens while Lizzy headed into the house to assure the men that she was not in the way. The old horse stall they put the chickens in wouldn't be practical in the long run, but the birds would be safe until they could be relocated to a more permanent location. The poor farmer felt a pang of regret as he left the animals behind, even more so than when he and Lizzy had looked on their ramshackle house for the last time.

The little girl was waiting at the table when the two men went inside to settle up the payment for the birds. Her father had half expected to find Lizzy munching on a biscuit or sipping on a cup of cool tea when he entered. Instead, his daughter sat upright in her chair with her hands in her lap with a look of unease on her face. The little girl looked for all the world as if she had just been scolded by a teacher at school.

"You just have a seat there while I go get my ledger," Bixby instructed. Although Ezra had always felt a little intimidated by the successful and outspoken rancher, he did not fail to notice that the old man had avoided making any kind of eye-contact since the two had exchanged greetings a few minutes before.

"I'm awful thirsty, Pa," Lizzy complained.

"I know, honey," her father replied, and he honestly did. It had been a long and unhappy walk to the Bixby ranch that morning as their sore feet and dry throats could attest to. "I'm sure old Nan will fetch us something to wet our whistles before we head out."

"I don't think so," the little girl admitted.

"Why's that?"

"Old Nan just smiled at me when I came in and walked away."

Ezra scratched under his chin, not really sure what his daughter was driving at. "That sounds like her," he explained. "She's probably fixing us something nice right now."

Lizzy shook her head. "No, sir. It was the *way* she smiled. It wasn't nice like she

241

did it before. She looked," the little girl scrunched up her face as she struggled to put her unease into words, "wrong! That's the best way I can put it."

"She's probably just feeling a little under the weather," Ezra explained. "She's not a spring chicken like yourself, pumpkin."

"No she's not," Bixby said, his unexpected voice causing both of his guests to start. "And I'd thank you not to pester her today. You're welcome to take some water from the well when our business is finished, though. Don't let it never be said that I'd turn a man and child out of my house without so much as a cup of water." The old man smiled as he said this, giving Ezra a good sense of what his daughter must have been talking about with regards to Nan's unsettling expression.

"That's mighty kind of you, sir, and much appreciated."

"Bah!" the rancher dismissed the praise. Despite the relative coolness of the house, a fat drop of sweat rolled down Bixby's forehead and splashed onto the rough surface of the table. "Now what say we settle our affairs and get you two on your way to a better life?"

"Amen," Ezra agreed. His own smile was a bit nervous, but still genuine for all that.

Bixby opened his ledger, a battered leather bound tome filled with waxy yellow pages. "So you've traded me what, seven birds today?"

"Eight," Lizzy piped up.

The rancher nodded as he jotted the number down. "Eight. Of course." Bixby ran his finger down a column on the opposite page before stopping on a certain figure and looking up to his guest. "I'm thinking a fair price for you would be two dollars apiece for the hens and one more for the pullet. That'd be," he paused to do the math in his head, "fifteen total. I was gonna throw together some things that I thought you and the girl could take along to wherever it is you're headed—where is that exactly?"

"Denver," Ezra replied.

"Denver? Never been there myself, but as good a place as any, I reckon." The rancher set his pencil down in the center of the ledger. "As I was saying, I was going to throw together some old things for you, but I just plumb forgot. Probably nothing you would want to haul around anyway."

Ezra shook his head. "Fifteen dollars is more than fair, Mr. Bixby. It's not much to set off on, but cash in my pocket is a damn sight better than pulling a pallet full of squawking birds."

"Truer words were never spoken, Mr. James," the old rancher agreed as he stuck out his hand.

Ezra took the proffered appendage and gave it a hardy shake. "My daughter and I are mighty obliged for your hospitality."

"Nonsense," the old man dismissed the praise. "Just let me write up a bank note for you and you can be on your way."

"A note?" the chicken farmer asked.

Bixby looked across the table at him and frowned slightly. "Is there something wrong with a note?"

Ezra shifted uncomfortably in his seat. "Not from you, sir. Not usually, that is. But Lizzy and I wanted to be on our way today and the coach don't take nobody to nowhere on credit."

"Of course," the rancher agreed. "A bank note is no good for traveling on, now is it?" He pushed away from the table and stood up. "I do keep some cash on hand but not all in one place. People with sticky fingers sometimes come through so I don't like to keep my valuables all together. I'm sure you understand."

Although Ezra had never in his life had enough valuables to squirrel away in more than one place, he nodded his vague understanding of the situation.

The old man's expression turned apologetic. "Now I trust you like my own kin, Mr. James, but still I'd be obliged if you would step outside while I procure your funds. A secret isn't much of a secret if I don't keep it to myself, after all."

When the two guests stood up and began making their way to the front door, Bixby stopped them. "Why don't you head out back and have some of that water I promised you. I won't be long, and you just drink as much as your bellies will hold in the meantime."

The invitation was as welcome a one as the thirsty pair had ever heard. They didn't need to be asked twice and quickly found themselves on the back porch looking at the faded stone cylinder that was the Bixby ranch's main source of water. It seemed to beckon to them from across the yard.

"Why did Mr. Bixby hide his money?" Lizzy asked in a hushed voice, a little worried that the old man might hear her and take some offense.

"To keep it safe from bandits," the girl's father explained in a half-joking way. Still, it seemed a little odd that a man with the resources of Edward Bixby would consider a sum like fifteen dollars to be too large to keep all in one place. It didn't really concern him, however, as Ezra had learned that people with money were just a different sort altogether.

Lizzy seemed satisfied by the explanation and rushed over to the well before quickly pushing the wooden planks aside to take in a deep breath of cool damp air. Without waiting for her father, the little girl started pulling the rope that hung into the opening and was dismayed to discover that there was no bucket tied to the end.

"Looks like I'll have to tie you up by your feet and send you down with a cup," Ezra said as he saw the look of surprised disappointment on his daughter's face.

"Pa!" the girl protested through a sour-puss face.

"Okay. Okay." Ezra held up his hands in mock surrender. "I'm sure there's a bucket around here somewhere." Though his tone was light, the man's thirst had become a good deal more intense now that the water was so tantalizingly close.

Lizzy looked to be about to offer some suggestion and then stopped with her mouth half open. Instead of speaking, she pointed back to the house where old Nan stood wearing an enormous bonnet and holding a battered tin bucket in her gnarled right hand.

Ezra followed his daughter's gaze to the old Indian woman and he nodded in greeting. "Good day to you, ma'am. We were just looking for that bucket you got there."

Nan said nothing but hoisted the dull metal object in front of her as if to confirm that it was really what the man in the yard wanted. When Ezra nodded again and started moving towards her, Nan made her way into the yard and met him half way.

"Guess I'll have to tie this back on," Ezra smiled as he took the bucket and turned his back on the old woman. "I ain't too handy with knots, but I'll see if I can't figure something out."

"Let me try, Pa," Lizzy offered, but she backed away when she saw that the Indian woman had continued to make her way all the way to the edge of the well and was peering inside. The child was clearly uneasy with Nan's presence, but her father was too preoccupied to notice.

"I got it, hon," the man said without looking away from his task. Working the frayed rope in loops around the thin wire handle was simple enough, but securing a good knot had proven to be more difficult than Ezra had thought. After a few tries, he stood up from the bucket and wiped the sweat from his sun-reddened forehead in a gesture of resignation.

"Pardon me, ma'am, but could you…" the rest of his request faded in his mouth as he got a good long look at the face within the bonnet, now only inches away from his own.

It was Nan, more or less, but her eyes were so wide that the irises seemed to shrink away to pinpoints amidst the marbled-veined whites. Her grin was equally as ghastly, a crimson gash filled with crooked yellow bits of bone that hardly resembled the teeth they had once been. It was as if the Indian woman's kindly old face had been cut away and stretched over something so terrible that it could not show itself all at once.

Lizzy began to pull on her father's arm, but the horrorstruck widower could not tear his gaze away from the woman in front of him. He watched in dumb fascination while the already unnerving orifices of her face stretched and distorted as if a shadow were struggling to remove itself from a suit that was two sizes too small. The woman's eyes rolled up and dropped away into darkness and dozens of pencil-thin tendrils poured out of Nan's nostrils and mouth and began to probe the air only a thumb's width from the chicken farmer's gaping expression.

Ezra would have screamed to high heaven (and in his mind he already was) but before the sound could escape his chest, the Nan-thing's arm lashed out like a whip. With a sickening crunch, the blow smashed him across the side of his skull with enough force to sever the vertebrae holding it in place. There had never been any hope of Ezra surviving the sudden assault and the man's head flopped obscenely to the side while his limbs stiffened and twitched. After a few nightmarish seconds, his lifeless body crashed into the ground at his daughter's feet.

Lizzy found the voice her father could not.

The little girl screamed so loudly and so piercingly that her throat felt as if it were shredding from the effort. She screamed and she flailed her arms wildly in front of her while the creature that wore Nan's skin held its arms out to embrace Lizzy's body to its own obscene form.

Ezra's daughter turned to run but quickly found her feet tangled in the rope her father had been holding the moment before. The ground rushed up and knocked the wind from her already straining lungs. The screaming came to an abrupt stop as the little girl lay wheezing painfully on her side. Her father's hand was just a few

249

inches away and she grasped it desperately in her own, hoping upon hope that he was somehow just faking, playing one of the little games he liked to tease her with. That was the thought that ran through her mind as the first of the inky tendrils brushed her cheek.

Where it made contact with her fragile white flesh, it burned.

Chapter Seventeen

The cowboy listened to all of this without expression.

"When the screaming stopped," Bixby explained, "I knew it was over."

"So your Indian woman's been some sort of monster all these years," the cowboy asked, "and you didn't notice?"

The old rancher had told the story in a mostly matter-of-fact way, as if was talking about mending a fence or stocking up on supplies for the winter. Just then, however, real ire came back into his voice. "Don't be stupid!" he spat. "Nan was the kindest and most gentle creature to ever grace this earth."

"Then maybe I don't understand."

"Neither do I," the rancher admitted. "Not entirely, at least. I found Nan laying out by the well the same night you came calling with your addle-brained idea to dig a well. I was spooked at first, but she looked like she just took a little tumble. I rushed out to her and when I turned her over I could see something was wrong." The old man paused. "No, that ain't really right. She looked mostly the same then, but I could *feel* something was wrong. When her eyes met mine there was something empty in them. And although Nan had always had strong hands, I thought her fingers were going to dig clean through my shoulders when I tried to help her up."

The old man dropped his head into his face. One minute he had been nearly a caricature—a stage villain about to twirl his mustache—and the next he was transformed into an almost pitiable mourner grieving over his lost love. The illusion was thin, however, as the cowboy envisioned the rancher watching that little girl and her father fall prey to some ungodly abomination from the safety of his kitchen.

"When that thing talked to me," Bixby continued, "it didn't use no words, just pictures in my head. I could see—" his voice caught in his throat, "I could see Nan's face when she died. I could even feel a little of her fear and pain."

The cowboy looked on as the rancher struggled with his conflicting emotions, and it nearly turned his stomach. Still, he had discovered that a man often learned more just by waiting than from trying to figure out which questions to ask, and so he waited. Sure enough, after another moment, Bixby got ahold of himself and the cowboy was rewarded for his patience.

"The thing was insane. Mad in a way I don't think a human being can really understand. There was a rage that made my brain feel like it was going to crack clean out of my skull. If you could know that, could *feel* that kind of madness stab into you, you wouldn't judge me for what I did."

Scott very much doubted that, but he kept the observation to himself. "Go on," he encouraged. Though the pain in the back of his head was still very real, it no longer had the same hold on him. The cowboy was ready to move, he believed, once he had all the information he could swallow.

"Now it was hungry." The old man began to chew absently on his thumbnail as he thought back. "It had been sleeping for an awfully long time, like a bear in the winter."

"Hibernation," Scott offered.

"Yeah. Hiber...whatever. Anyway," Bixby continued, "I was next up on the menu if I didn't find it something better. I tried to offer it cattle, but it had had its fill of the beasts of the earth. My poor sweet Nan, it seemed, had given it a taste for something new, something that hadn't been around the last time it was awake. At first I thought of some of the boys on the ranch, but if one of them disappeared, the rest would start asking questions. But—"

"But nobody would get too worked up about a down-on-his-luck widower and his little girl," the cowboy finished for him. "They were two folks that had wandered off to find a better life and just never bothered to write. And," he added, "maybe you could add a drifting ranch hand who had worn out his welcome to the list. No real loss to anybody, so no harm done, right?"

"That's right," Bixby agreed, almost eagerly. "You understand, don't you?"

"What I understand," the cowboy said, "is that you used to be a good man. But you've seen terrible things, and they done broke your mind like a hammer to a block of ice."

The young man got to his feet, his legs holding strong this time. "Of course, I'm not here to clasp your hand and mete out forgiveness for you turning into a weak and selfish fraud of a human being," the cowboy explained. "You'll have to ask for that from whatever god will have you, if such a one even exists. But I do have one last question for you."

The old man looked on blankly, as if the venom in the cowboy's words held no sting for him. "What's that?"

"The little girl. Did you see her die?"

The rancher nearly answered, the breath in his lungs seemed almost eager to do so, but then fear clouded his face and the words melted into a shudder. The old man's gaze briefly turned in the direction of the well before he silently shook his head.

"That will have to do then," the cowboy said, and fired a single bullet into the brain of Edward Bixby before dropping the weapon smoothly back into its holster.

A mind filled with terror and shame was suddenly snuffed out like a candle—another life gone from the earth forever. The thought made Scott feel sick to even think upon it and he was worried that he might fall again as black spots came back in to block up his vision. He gripped the back of the chair with whatever strength he could muster and took a deep breath to calm his nerves. The scent of the onions on the table filled his nostrils at that moment and he knew he would never be able to eat that particular vegetable again.

The cowboy may have been cool enough when he pulled the trigger, but he had never killed a man before, at least not one that he knew of, and it didn't come easy to him. Sure, he had shot at some dangerous hombres in the past and even managed to wing a few, but that was always in self-defense and always ended with one party or the other riding away to fight another day. In those cases, the loser's heart may have been pounding with fear or rage, but at least it had still been beating.

In Scott's mind, what he had just done was an act of murder; gunning down an unarmed man in his own home. Bixby might have had it coming, but the cowboy didn't see that he was any more fit to dole out such irrevocable justice than he was for offering absolution. It was something that would take time, and maybe more than a little whisky, to truly come to grips with. Even so, the cowboy doubted he would ever learn to be entirely comfortable with himself again, knowing what he was ultimately capable of.

But he wouldn't let the old man's death go to waste. Scott had not shot Bixby out of anger so much as necessity. If there was any chance to save Lizzy, he could not afford to be looking over his shoulder in case the crazed and vengeful old bastard decided to come after him or, worse, to call all of his ranch hands to a manhunt. The darkness of the well was waiting for him, and it held more than enough dangers of its own.

Clearing his mind of everything but the task at hand, the cowboy quickly located and grabbed a lantern from the adjoining room. He would have felt better to have a rifle slung over his back but, contrary to what he had originally thought, there was none to be found. Bixby surely kept a weapon somewhere in his house, but Lizzy's time on this earth, if she still had any, was running down too quickly to afford a search.

The back door banged shut behind him as the cowboy made his way to the edge of the well. The boards were already moved aside, the rope hanging down a challenge to climb for anyone foolish enough to try to plumb the darkness within. The cowboy clenched the lantern between his teeth and started making his way down before his fear could overcome that prerequisite foolishness. The earth eagerly swallowed him whole.

The wire handle pulled painfully at his jaw, but to lose it would be to succumb to failure from the outset. The cowboy may have been brave enough to face whatever terrors lurked beneath the surface of the Bixby ranch, but not without a light. Thankfully, the decent was fairly brief and soon the cowboy found himself thigh-deep in a rippling pool of cool well water.

The lantern, now comfortably in hand, showed Scott to be in a small chamber not much bigger than a pantry. He had just enough room to stand upright and turn around, but there was no dry land to be seen. The water seemed to be flowing in from what the cowboy guessed was the north toward a narrow crevice in the opposite wall, and so that was where he made his way.

The would-be hero quickly found himself in the grip of panic as his gun belt caught on the rough wall of the crevice as he was trying to force his way through. The image of being trapped within the narrow confines of the rock walls flashed into his mind and he could not even count all of the ways he suddenly realized he could die there. To his surprise, however, it was Bixby's death that got him through the worst of his sudden, crippling fear.

A little voice in the back of the cowboy's mind told him that he deserved to die down there in the hard, stony womb of the earth and, in that brief moment of resignation, his body relaxed enough that he almost fell through to the opposite side. He hadn't realized how tense his body had been and he understood that his nerves would only be a continued hindrance if he didn't keep them in check. "Don't be such little priss," he whispered to himself as he straightened his belt and surveyed the next section of cave. There would be time for him to wallow in self-pity once his work was done. If he were truly destined to die down there, he doubted that giving in to fear or guilt would make his fate any easier to face.

Thankfully, there was a small bank next to the river on the other side of the crevice and the cowboy was able to exit the stream and set the lantern down long enough to pour the water from his boots. Taking advantage of the opportunity, Scott drew a fresh cartridge from a thick leather loop on his belt and opened the chamber of his six-shooter. The empty casing within stared up at him accusingly, but he plucked it out and replaced it before he could let his guilt unman him any further.

His weapon fully loaded and back in its holster, the cowboy straightened up and followed the edge of the cavern deeper into the earth. A few times he had to step back into the water to go around some unexpected jut of rock, but he was grateful that the cold liquid never reached over the top of his boots. The cowboy dreaded the idea of the sleepily moving water becoming a dangerous torrent as it had where he had met it in the cavern that Lizzy had shown him, an event that seemed like an eternity ago, but Scott would deal with that obstacle when the time came.

Unfortunately, it came sooner than he would have liked. He had been walking for the better part of an hour when he heard the familiar rush of water against stone echoing ahead of him. He had the choice of following the main tunnel towards the unwelcome sound or trying to squeeze himself into one of the various crevices that occasionally opened along the way. There was no good way to continue, but facing the underground river seemed preferable to being trapped again or tumbling into some black abyss by plunging ahead where he could not clearly see.

A few more minutes of careful navigation over slippery rocks found the cowboy on the edge of the underground torrent. The echoing roar was almost deafening in the otherwise soundless confines of the cavern. The light of the lantern reflected back in shifting yellow ribbons from the surface of the water, but it could not penetrate far enough into the darkness to illuminate the opposite bank.

The water was not likely as all-fired deep as it seemed, the cowboy figured, but the force of it was still quite impressive. He remembered clearly how it had nearly jerked the bucket from his hand the first time he had tried to draw from it. What was more, that water was significantly colder than the pleasantly cool stream Scott had been following up until that point. If the river's current didn't pull him under or smash his head into an unseen stalactite, cramping muscles could easily finish the job. All that assumed that there was even an opposite bank to be reached in the first place, rather than another featureless stone wall.

I can't turn back, the cowboy thought to himself, though he could not conceive of a way to move forward. He spent the next few minutes feeling around the walls for hand holds and scouring the surface of the water in case one area appeared shallower than another. It did not take long, however, for him to realize the futility of his search.

"God *DAMN* it!" he cried out, his voice rising above the roar of the rushing water and echoing back faintly from the darkness.

"That you, cowboy?" a tiny voice suddenly called out from the unseen distance.

At first, Scott assumed his fevered mind was playing games with him until he saw the familiar glow of an oil lantern growing steadily larger on what had to be the opposite bank of the river. A human shadow eventually emerged standing behind the light, but the cowboy could not make out who it was.

"Who's asking?" Scott called out in reply, his hand dropping to the handle of his gun.

"Why don't you take a guess," the familiar voice drawled, almost drowned out by the river's ceaseless rumble.

"Wayne?" The cowboy was dumbfounded. "Holy Christ, man! What are you doing over there?"

"Same thing as you, I reckon," came the reply. "Sticking my damn fool nose where it's got no business being."

The cowboy choked up a little, so relieved was he to know he was not alone down there. After a few more shouted questions and instructions, along with some frustrated attempts at catching the thrown end of a rope, Scott made his way across the water which, while swift and powerful, was mercifully only about as deep as the pool he had found himself in when he had first entered the well. It was also not as wide as the seemingly endless darkness had suggested. The cowboy realized that he might have been able to wade across without Wayne's help, but it was a dangerous and unwelcome gamble he was happy to avoid.

Once Scott was safely out of the water, the two men clasped hands in mutual gratitude. Wayne, as it turned out, had not been as cowed by Bixby's harsh words as the cowboy had thought. In fact, he had been downright furious. If there was something in the water that had poisoned his cousin, the ranch hand would be damned if he was going to be bullied into poking cows instead of trying to find the cause. Instead of doing as he had said, Wayne had almost immediately grabbed a lantern and some rope and headed back to the worksite.

"So you got here from the new well?" the cowboy asked.

"That I did," Wayne admitted. "I didn't know what I was going to find down here, sure as hell not you, but I had to at least take a look." The ranch hand wiped a finger under his thin nose. "Bixby's money might buy my time and muscle, but I'm pretty damned sure it didn't buy my soul."

The cowboy nodded his understanding, "I'm happier to see you than you know, Wayne, but you got to understand that once we get out of here, you might be sorry you found me."

The lanky man scratched at the back of his head. "Why is that? And what the hell are you doing down here anyway?"

"It would take too long to explain it to you right now, but let it suffice that little Lizzy might be down here and I'm not leaving until I know for sure."

"Lizzy?" Wayne asked incredulously. "What in tarnation would that little thing be doing down here? She and her pa ought to

263

be half way to wherever they were headed by now."

The cowboy shook his head. "They never left the ranch." He held up his hand before the other man could argue. "I know it sounds crazy, but although I'm pretty sure that Ezra is dead, I think that Lizzy might be alive somewhere down here. I don't know what shape she's in if she is, but I mean to find out." He paused to survey the new side of the river. "You see sign of any other people down here?"

Wayne thought back for a moment. "No sign of a little girl, though I did find something damn strange not far from here."

"What's that?" the cowboy asked, a nervous edge to his voice.

"I ain't quite sure, really. Looked like a woman's clothes, too large for a little girl I reckon, and maybe a horse skin."

"A horse skin?"

Wayne puckered his lips in thought. "It was a sort of brown pile that had a bunch of long black hair flowing out of one end. I don't know what else it could be. Though, to be honest, I didn't really get too close. The smell just about turned my guts inside out."

"Nan," the cowboy spat the word out like a curse.

The ranch hand barked out a laugh in reply. "You hit your head or something down here, cowboy? I can't say as I'd believe that old Nan was down here skinning horses."

"I think what you saw," Scott explained, "is what is left of Nan."

The mirth fled from Wayne's face as if it had been slapped off of it. "What's that now?"

The cowboy let out a sigh. It was clear that Wayne was going to need to know more if he was going to be of any help. He wasn't sure how much he should share, but Scott decided that he wasn't in a position to be picky about whom he could trust. "Bear with me for a minute," he tried to think of where to begin. "Now if you came in from the new well, then we must be somewhere west of the cavern. Am I right?"

Wayne nodded his agreement, though he did not really understand how that question related to old Nan. "I should think so. We ain't but 10 minutes from where we was digging yesterday. Why? Where are you coming from?"

"Bixby's place," Scott explained. "I've been down here for a while."

Wayne whistled appreciatively. "I should say so."

"Why did you head this way?" the cowboy asked. "Was this the only open direction from where you came in?"

"No," the ranch hand replied. "I figured that if something was making the water sour, the smart thing would be to follow it to the source. I heard the sound of the river so that's the way I started."

"Smart man," Scott noted.

Wayne smirked. "Don't need to read no school book to know that much, hombre."

"There's nothing back the way I came," the cowboy said. "It's pretty much just more of what you see here, so let's you and me try the other direction. I'll tell you what I can while we walk back to where you came. There shouldn't be too many surprises before then." He paused for a moment. "I warn you though, if you didn't think I was crazy before, you just might before I'm done talking."

Wayne stopped in his tracks for a moment and eyed Scott thoughtfully in the yellow glow of the lantern. The cowboy seemed uneasy in general, but the grim set of his jaw said that he was not in a mind for foolishness or leg pulling. Whatever the young drifter had to say, he was dead serious about it.

"Fair enough, partner," Wayne answered. "You've got my full attention."

Chapter Eighteen

The cowboy started his tale slowly, talking about how Bixby and he had both had run-ins with some kind of strange *animal*—once when the old rancher had been young, and again a few days before when the cowboy had come into town. Wayne listened patiently without interrupting with any of the questions that must have been swimming around in his head. The ranch hand seemed quite willing to accept that there were mysterious things in the world that he did not know about, including dangerous animals that lived under the earth.

Before he could get much deeper into the tale, a warm rotten smell penetrated the cool earthiness of the tunnel. The cowboy quickly pulled his faded bandana up over his nose, though it did little to block the permeating odor. The two men stopped and gazed upon the pile of remains that Wayne had mistaken for horse skin. The dress and bonnet were clearly Nan's, the cowboy recognized, and what lay tangled in them would have been enough to give him nightmares if he had not had enough fuel for them already.

The cowboy poked at the pile with the tip of his boot, flipping it over and revealing another unwelcome discovery. Although he could not be sure what Ezra had been wearing when he died, Scott guessed that the newly uncovered mound of bloody cloth, punctuated here and there with a jutting white knob or shard of bone, were all that remained of the down-on-his luck chicken farmer.

"Lizzy is truly alone in this world now," the cowboy said before swearing softly under his breath.

Wayne hunkered down to investigate more carefully.

"You say some kind of animal did this?" The ranch hand, apparently more accustomed to and better able to handle the odor of fresh slaughter, pulled a knife from his belt and began to probe the pile of remains. A look of terror and fascination replaced his usual placid and disinterested expression.

"Something like that," the cowboy admitted just before he felt his gorge rise and drop in quick succession. "Why don't we go?" he almost pleaded. "There's nothing we can do for them just now."

Wayne nodded and made the sign of the cross as he got to his feet. "Yeah, I suppose not."

The rest of the cowboy's tale poured out of him a little easier after the grisly discovery. Now that Wayne knew beyond a shadow of a doubt that there was something sinister going on in the caverns, it seemed easier to lay everything out on the table. The story continued as they passed under the newly dug well and finally, into the uncharted territory of the westward leading cavern. Scott told his companion everything he thought was relevant, stopping short of describing the creatures that he and Bixby had encountered and leaving out the small detail of the old man's death.

"Mother of God," Wayne muttered to himself as the cowboy reached the end of his account. "I thought you said you were going to be straight with me. Hell! I could practically see it in your eyes."

Scott came to a halt and eyed the ranch hand cautiously. "What do you mean? I meant every word I said."

"Not *every* word," the ranch hand clarified. "What I mean is that there ain't no animal like what you've been talking about. I know you think I'm none too bright, but I ain't a damned fool, neither."

There was no heat in the man's voice, so the cowboy continued to listen. "Go on."

"Shadows that sound like snakes and eat men whole? Creatures that can get inside a woman's skin and walk her around like a puppet? Does that sound like any animal you know?"

"Well no, Wayne. But I—" Scott found himself cut off.

"But you thought that an animal was the closest thing I could understand, right?" Wayne shook his head. "You and Allen can be so damned pleased with your learned ways sometimes that it's a wonder you even bother talking to us common folk."

The cowboy was surprised by the fervor in his companion's voice as he spoke. "People like you think that because you read a few more books that the rest of us got nothing but tumbleweeds knocking around in our heads." He poked at his temple with a gloved finger to illustrate the point. "Did it ever occur to you that if you had told your story to one of those book-learned men you think so highly of, that he might just say you were just plain cracked? That maybe he'd leave you down here to chase your shadows, if'n you could even get him to follow you down here in the first place?"

"I reckon that's possible," the cowboy admitted a little sheepishly.

"Well, all that learning might make your mind bigger, but it sure does close it up right fast, too, sometimes. Ain't that so?" He didn't wait for an answer. "The truth is that I *know* there is evil in the world, and not just evil men. It might bother me to learn that there was some nameless horror sleeping under my feet all this time, but it don't surprise me in the least."

The cowboy, however, was quite surprised. "I'm genuinely sorry Wayne," he apologized. "I shouldn't have looked, down on you as I did."

"You ain't the first," the ranch hand admitted, the preaching tone fading from his voice, "and I can't say as I don't bring it on myself sometimes. But let's leave that aside and you start telling me everything. And I mean *every*thing."

Finally the cowboy did just that. He poured out every detail no matter how unsettling or shameful it might have been. There was a good chance he was going to die down in those caverns and it did him some real good to let it all out with a level of honesty that he didn't think he could have reached even with Bixby, a man who had known exactly what kind of fear and uncertainty the cowboy was talking about.

Wayne listened patiently until the end and said, "You done what was right."

271

"About what?" the cowboy asked.

"About everything, including the old man." The ranch hand turned his head and spit. "Bixby weren't Bixby no more and you put him down before he could lose any more of what made him a good man. You see that, right?"

The cowboy frowned. "That's what I think in my head, but not how I feel in here." He tapped at the center of his chest.

"That'll take time, more than we got to spare at the moment, but it will happen." Wayne started heading west again, his lantern held high in front of him. "If Lizzy is out there somewhere, I don't guess she's too happy about being kept waiting. Women are like that."

At first the cowboy felt ashamed of how he had approached Wayne with his story, but the sense of relief he felt for having spoken freely was immeasurable. For the first time since he had pulled the trigger in Bixby's kitchen, he truly felt that he was doing the right thing instead of just hoping that he was. As Wayne had said, there would be time to deal with the cost of his actions once the dust had settled. Until then, there was a single goal to focus on.

Wayne continued walking in silence and the cowboy followed closely behind. More than once, the sound of a shifting stone or distant echo sent his hand reaching for the familiar grip of his pistol, but Scott resisted the urge to draw it from the holster. Though the weapon was a comfort to him, it wouldn't do to have it go off unexpectedly in such close and unpredictable quarters.

The minutes passed by and progress was gratefully unimpeded by any unexpected barriers. Just as before, the underground stream sometimes overtook the path along the banks, but their boots could not have been any wetter, and so dealing with the cool water was more of an issue of moving quietly than staying dry. There were points where the ceiling dropped so low and the path narrowed so greatly that it was necessary, and occasionally terrifying, to crawl and shimmy to make progress, however. Unpleasant as that was, the way was never blocked by the jutting points of rock or fallen stones the cowboy expected to come upon around every curve.

The notion that the path had been made so clear and easy by some rampaging shadowy horror was too unnerving to focus on and so the cowboy decided that his unspoken gratitude for their swift forward momentum was sufficient. Eventually, though, Wayne came to a stop and commented on their location.

"We've got to be getting close to town," he whispered. Although they had not seen nor heard sign of any living creatures other than themselves, a foreboding sense that they were not alone pervaded the twisting confines of the tunnel.

The cowboy nodded his agreement. "If the path don't branch off someplace soon, our way'll be blocked by the cave-in."

"What do you want to do, then?"

"Not much else we *can* do but keep going," Scott replied matter-of-factly, though he felt the dread of stopping cold at a dead end pressing in on his chest. He didn't know what was worse: facing the thing in the darkness or facing his fate back up in the light. The most unnerving part was that it was still his unwavering plan to do both.

At least the fear of being trapped against a cave-in turned out to be unfounded, as the tunnel reached an unexpectedly sudden (but blessedly welcome) fork. Wayne came to a halt and held up his hand to signal to the cowboy that he should do likewise. Both men raised their lanterns to see which of the two choices might serve them better and, luck again on their side, the choice was an easy one.

To the right the stream flowed steadily on, no doubt continuing into the debris that entombed the creature the cowboy had unwittingly stumbled upon a few days earlier. It felt like a lifetime ago that the young drifter and his horse had had the misfortune of wandering into Drum Hollow, but it was still too soon for the cowboy to want to return to the site of his first attempted good deed.

The left path sloped downward and, if their sense of direction could be trusted, south of the town. How far the two men had left to go was anybody's guess, however, and so the cowboy reluctantly snuffed out his lantern to save fuel. Though Scott and his companion had been traveling close enough to each other that a single light was sufficient, having a lantern of his own to carry had been a source of comfort. Its sudden absence increased the cowboy's sense of dread and, as a result, he spent the next several minutes traveling with his hand unconsciously gripping the handle of his revolver, though with no more intention of drawing it than before. It was simply a matter of replacing one comfort for another.

"Hold up a sec," Wayne whispered. The ranch hand had stopped so suddenly that Scott ran into him, sending a small cascade of pebbles tumbling down the wall. The rush of the underground stream was so far behind them that the new sound echoed with unexpected volume and the cowboy hissed at his blunder. The unnatural-seeming silence quickly returned, however, bringing with it equal parts relief and unease.

Before the two men, the earth opened into a cavern so wide that the light of Wayne's lantern could not discern the extent of the surrounding walls. In a way, it was a welcome respite from the cramped confines they had been making their way through, as the men finally had the space to stand side-by-side and stretch the kinks out of their backs. However, it also meant that they were leaving the relative security of being able to see and touch the walls and ceiling at any time, rather than blundering into the black unknown.

The cowboy placed his left hand against the lip of the entrance and took a step in that direction before motioning for Wayne to do the same. As long as they stuck to the wall in that fashion, Scott reasoned, they would avoid stumbling blindly into a bottomless abyss or, almost as bad, completely losing their sense of direction and wandering into another of any possible unseen exits.

Slowly and carefully, the two men made their way forward. The cowboy continued to lead while Wayne held the lantern above him from behind. The lanky man's arm trembled from the weight, but he dared not let it drop. The darkness of the cavern seemed to press down on the sphere of light created by the lantern, as if it were determined to snuff it out along with the two intruders who had the audacity to take refuge in it. Without realizing it, Wayne had become as concerned about protecting the lantern as he was with finding the little girl.

There was no way to know how big the shadowy expanse of the room was. The men could have been ten inches from the next wall or ten yards. The sound of their breathing and the faint shuffle of their feet seemed inexplicably loud in the tomblike silence of the enclosure and the sensation that a silent predator lay in wait for them was almost palpable. Neither of the would-be rescuers dared to speak out of some vague dread that to do so might invite an answer from something in the darkness.

Time seemed to have lost its meaning within the lightless belly of the earth, but eventually the cowboy spotted something to his right, just at the edge of the lantern's glow. He took ahold of Wayne's wrist and guided it until the lamp revealed a faded blue bundle that contrasted sharply against the hard yellow rock of the floor.

"It's her," Wayne's whisper was like the hiss of a specter in the darkness, but the cowboy did not hear him. Already the other man was on his knees cradling the limp body against his chest.

Dark Rivers

Chapter Nineteen

Lizzy's body was cold and soaking wet, coated from head to toe in the same tan and rust-colored dust that Scott and Wayne had accumulated during their journey to the cavern. The little girl's arms and legs were marred by dozens of small abrasions and there was an ugly gash running from the edge of her scalp to the corner of her right eye. The rough and muddy trek through the subterranean tunnels had left Lizzy little more than a sodden lump with blood and grit dried into a mask across half her face. It was almost more than the cowboy could bear.

We're too late, the cowboy realized. There had never been any real chance of saving Lizzy at all, it seemed. The loathsome creature had dragged the little girl like it was an angry child with a ragdoll during its flight through the tunnels, battering her against passing obstacles before discarding her lifeless form once it became too much of a burden.

Scott clutched the girl to his chest and rested his chin atop her filthy hair. "I'm so sorry," he muttered as he began to slowly rock back and forth on the cold ground.

Wayne looked on dumbfounded, somehow unable to fully accept that they had failed. He had never been the heroic sort but, if he had ever wished for anything in his life, he wished that they had been able to be heroes for that little girl. He wished for it so much, in fact, that he almost let the shifting shadows convince him that he had seen her fingers twitch. Then he saw it again.

"She ain't dead," he said softly, more to himself than to his companion.

At first the cowboy did not hear, but when he heard Wayne repeat the statement he looked up at him, his pleading eyes red with unshed tears.

The ranch hand set the lantern on the ground and reached out to take one of the little girl's hands between his own. He rubbed it vigorously and smiled when it saw it redden with still-flowing blood. Lizzy was in bad shape, no one could argue to the contrary, but deep down in her broken body her heart was still beating and that meant that there was a chance to get her to the surface alive. There was no saying as to whether or not her body would recover from its recent abuse, of course, but just the possibility was enough for the moment.

The cowboy almost laughed with relief, but he knew just as well as his companion that it was too early to celebrate. "Let's get her out of here," he said in a voice that sounded a lot steadier than it felt.

"What about the thing that took her?" Wayne asked. "It's still down here somewhere."

"That can wait," Scott declared grimly. "Keeping Lizzy alive is our priority now."

Wayne nodded his understanding as he used his thumb to brush a bit of crusted blood and earth from the little girl's cheek. It was a tender gesture that bespoke of the man's gentle nature better than any words and the cowboy realized that there was probably no man on earth he would rather have had helping him at that moment.

Scott was reflecting upon how much people could surprise you as the lanky ranch hand reached out for his light again. Just before his fingers brushed the thin wire of the handle, however, Wayne suddenly and silently disappeared into the darkness behind him.

"Wayne?" the cowboy asked. He waited a brief moment for a reply that did not come before asking again. Hearing nothing, Scott reluctantly laid Lizzy back on the cold ground and stood squinting into the darkness until blackness seemed to shift and purple from the strain.

"If you can hear me, Wayne," the cowboy instructed, "Try to—"

His words were cut off by a wet tearing sound followed by a hot splash of liquid across his face and torso. Scott instantly recognized the coppery tang of blood and screamed.

"WAYNE!"

The pearl-handle revolver was in the cowboy's grip, his left hand fanning the hammer, as six shots exploded into the darkness before the first drop of gore could fall from the shooter's chin. The cannon-like echo deafened him and the smoke burned his eyes, but still the cowboy had seen and now there was no unseeing it.

Though the bullets had done little more than ricochet dangerously off the cavern walls, the flash of the power had revealed a hideous black man-thing flailing about in indescribably alien motions. That much alone the cowboy could might have stomached, but something even more terrible had burned its unwelcome way into his brain along with it. It was the sight of the upper third of Wayne, a man Scott was realizing could have been a true and lifelong friend, tumbling through the air with a slack-jawed expression of shock on his face. That was what threatened to sever the thin thread of sanity the young wanderer's mind was desperately clinging to.

The cowboy screamed again, but this time the sound was without words. It was a primal scream of fear and rage and he poured it into the darkness until his throat burned and the tendons in his neck felt as if they would snap from the strain. Eventually his throat could take no more and the sound ended in a choked sob.

"You come out, you sick *fuck*!" Scott rasped out his challenge. "Come out where I can see you!" His knees trembled slightly, but his hands remained steady. Six empty shells rained out from the open chamber of the revolver and were replaced with fresh rounds—the last in his gunbelt. With a practiced snap of his wrist, the cowboy was armed again but it did not make him feel brave or strong.

Instead the drifter, deep down in the black bowels of the world, felt numb. Wayne was gone, Lizzy lay dying at his feet, and the glow of the lantern did little more than make the cowboy an easy target. Dying on his feet with his gun in his hand suddenly seemed like the best he could hope for.

With no real expectation of getting out alive, the cowboy's mind was focused keenly on the moment. There was no longer any future or past, only the darkness and the something that lurked within it. The ringing in his ears from the rapid fire shots faded away and Scott could feel subtle currents of air shifting coolly across his skin where before he had only felt stifling stillness. That's when he closed his eyes.

We will die together, you and I. The thought slid smoothly through his conscious mind like a red ribbon floating on the surface of an ebony pool. The mental declaration was heard, he knew, by an alien mind that danced along the edges of his own consciousness. The adrenaline was gone and the cowboy felt as if his body, now as still as the stone it stood upon, had simply sprouted from the earth.

He heard a soft rustling, yet the barrel of the old gun, though unseen, remained steady. It was Lizzy, the cowboy was sure, but he was in too single-minded of a state to consider that any movement on her part was a good sign. Then, without warning, he turned forty-five degrees to his right and fired.

The ear-splitting blast of the gunshot was not enough to cover a swine-like shriek of pain that answered back just before an invisible rope of barbed flesh whipped out at the cowboy's neck. In a silken motion the sightless man shifted his weight to the right and fired again, miraculously managing to both dodge the attack and score another hit of his own.

The second shot hit truer than the first, eliciting not an angry bellow, but a soft bursting sound followed by a gurgling hiss. He fired a third and fourth time, again rewarded by the fleshy sound of hot lead meeting the cold black surface of the thing. There was a brief pause just before Scott heard the meaty thud of the creature's body dropping hard against the unforgiving cavern floor.

At last, the cowboy allowed himself to open his eyes and the world of light poured eagerly back into his mind. A gentle curl of smoke rose from the barrel of the weapon that remained pointed into the darkness and Lizzy still lay at his feet. Now the child's eyes were open, wide with shock in fact, but she was not staring at her rescuer. Her gaze was fixed on something just over his shoulder. The cowboy's body swung around to meet whatever the little girl had been looking at, revolver ready to empty its final two shots, but there was only more darkness.

Finally, he let his arm relax and drop to his side.

Scott's ears roared in pain and the cowboy wouldn't have been surprised if the right one wasn't bleeding from the way it throbbed. He moved his jaw back and forth to try to relieve some of the pressure and before he could ask Lizzy if she was alright, the world tilted and he was slammed painfully into the rocky ground while his gun jumped free of his grip.

The air whooshed out of the cowboy's lungs from the impact and the jagged floor of the cavern tore at his palms as he fought to free himself from iron grip of myriad black tendrils that were rapidly looping around his legs and torso. As he was flipped onto his back, Scott could see that the fleshy extensions varied in size from needle thin to as wide as a rattlesnake, all of them cinched so tightly against his body that he was sure that his knees would shatter as they ground against each other. If the constricting tendrils managed to reach as high as his arms, the cowboy knew, it was all over.

"Lizzy, grab my gun!" he called out in a voice weakened by the increasing pressure as well as from his previous emotional outburst.

The little girl only skittered away, however, managing to kick over the lantern in the process. The thought of grabbing the burning light and smashing it into his adversary, something that had proven effective in the past, went through the cowboy's mind, but his flailing arms and grasping fingers found nothing but emptiness when they reached out for it.

Again, a single thought came back to him. *We die together.*

Throwing his weight forward, the cowboy launched himself at the thing that grappled against him, moving into its bulk rather than continuing to pull away from it. The man's hands, tired and torn as they were, were still strong enough to reach into the shadowy form and fight to what was sure to be one hell of a bitter end.

The cowboy's left fist was quickly snatched up by a steely rope of flesh, the barbs of which sawed into his skin like a rusty blade. Unflinching, Scott's right hand continued forward and slid into a gritty pocket of flesh. The frayed edges of the opening suggested that it was a wound caused by one of the shots he had landed, and so the desperate cowboy thrust his arm in as deep as it would go.

It was cold inside the body of the beast, and lined with hard ridges like the gills of a fish. Scott felt a chill ride through him in a wave after his hand entered. Still his fingers clutched and tore until they were almost numb while the creature, so eager to

Eric Kerkove

crush the cowboy to its body only a moment ago, suddenly began trying to force him away. Finally, the hellish black thing succeeded in breaking free and tossing the haggard man away from itself, sending his battered body, now slick with a layer of unearthly gore, flying into the air.

There was a grim but satisfied grin on the cowboy's face as the wall of the cavern came crashing into him from behind. In his right hand, now almost completely without feeling, was a throbbing chunk of something dark and sticky. Behind the abominable pulsing object was a stream of torn flesh and stringy sinew that trailed back to the now and forever still form of the terrible black thing on the cavern floor.

Chapter Twenty

Aunt Jesse continued to fuss over the little girl who, while healing from her physical wounds, remained sullen even as the days turned to weeks. The older woman sat up and frowned. "You'd do yourself a world of good to get out and enjoy some sunshine today, Little Miss."

Lizzy's eyes met with those of her caretaker and she nodded. She was trying to be well, that much was clear, but some cuts just ran deeper than others. She would be alright, Jesse was sure, but it would take time.

Outside on the cabin porch, the cowboy was sitting on a bench and carefully oiling the disassembled pieces of his six-shooter, something he had taken to doing two and even three times a day during his stay with the widow and her son. Beside him, quietly smoking a pipe and staring out into the late afternoon sky, Allen sat in a rickety-looking rocking chair. The soldier was still a formidable site, but he had lost a good deal of weight during his time recovering from his bout with the tainted well water and his clothes hung off him like a scarecrow.

"You know my ma will take good care of her," Allen mentioned not for the first time. "She'll be safe here."

For a moment the cowboy said nothing, but then he set down the gleaming firing pin atop a thin sheet of grimy leather next to him and looked at his companion. "Ain't no place on this earth she'll be as safe as she deserves to be."

The big soldier frowned. "And yet somehow you think that she'd be better off traipsing through the plains with you instead of staying in a house with a woman to care for her and see that she rests her head every night in a warm bed with a full belly?" When there was no reply, he added, "What you do you think you can give her that's better than this?"

"Nothing," the cowboy admitted dully. "But I owe it to her daddy to take care of her. It's my fault she's got nobody now and I can't just drop her off on your doorstep and ride away." He knew it was a weak argument as soon as he spoke the words, however.

"Horse shit!" Allen exclaimed. "You ain't no more to blame for what happened to her pa than you are for the sun being hot at noon. I know you want to do right by Lizzy, but just 'cuz you feel you owe her something don't mean you're doing her right by trying to keep her at your side." He paused to take a long, slow draw from his pipe. "Your life ain't got no room for a little girl and you damn well know it."

The cowboy's head drooped. It was neither the first nor even the second time they had had that conversation and, just as before, he knew that the old soldier was right.

"Besides," Allen continued, "What are you going to do if the law catches up with you?"

That was the real kicker.

When the cowboy had come stumbling to the cabin with the little girl cradled in his arms, it had been dark enough to hide their passage from search parties and curious onlookers alike. Both figures were battered and covered with a mixture of blood and black ichor that stank so badly that Jesse had turned and retched when she met them at the door, but they had been welcomed in and sheltered all the same.

Hearing about Wayne had been the worst part, but somehow the soldier and his mother had believed the cowboy's fantastically grisly story of what had transpired beneath the earth. The good-natured ranch hand had not been the only one, it seemed, who believed that there were darker things in the world than most people were willing to admit to out loud.

To anyone in town or at the door, however, the soldier and his mother sternly denied any knowledge of the drifter—a friendless man whom the town's well respected saloon keeper had quickly accused of Old Man Bixby's murder. "I told that vagabond that he would hang," Albert had practically shouted at the sheriff. "He brought nothing but death and misery to this town and I demand that you see him brought to justice!" The sheriff, to his own credit, did what he could.

Lizzy's new caretakers also turned away the lawmen who came to make their inquiries early one evening. The myriad wounds, the black gore, and the haunted look in the little girl's eyes seemed enough to convince the widow and her son that sometimes the stuff of nightmares could seep into God's good earth and that letting the cowboy hang for facing down such evil would be like snuffing out one more precious candle in an endless darkness.

Despite the pair's best efforts, Scott was still a wanted man and he would likely remain that way for the rest of his days. The cowboy was both an outsider and a half-breed believed to have killed a well-established white man, something that would not easily be forgotten. Allen and his mother were taking a considerable risk allowing him to stay in their home, but they had insisted that it was only fair that the cowboy remain until he was sure that the little girl would be okay. That time had finally come, however, and Scott was finding it very difficult to leave Lizzy behind.

"Even if I left her here," the cowboy said more to himself than to the man next to him, "I won't leave Wayne down there to rot alongside that...that thing."

That was something that Allen readily agreed with. He could not stand the idea of his good-natured cousin being forgotten down in the belly of the earth like that. He had left too many men to the worms and the crows during his soldiering days, hoping (but never feeling too confident) that some weeping wife or sister would make their way to the blood soaked fields to find them. There was not even that little hope for Wayne. No one was going to brave the uncharted caverns to retrieve the remains of some unfortunate ranch hand who had been fool enough to disappear into a well he had helped dig himself. There was no one but themselves, and Allen, knowing full well that the cowboy wanted to do it by himself, was not about to shirk that duty.

"Whenever you're ready," the soldier stated.

The cowboy gave him a look of annoyance before sighing in resignation. "I guess there's no changing your mind, eh?"

"Damn straight there's not," Allen agreed.

Windkicker seemed ready—eager even—for an evening stroll. The astute animal had made its way onto Jesse's property only a few days earlier, apparently having abandoned his new owner to wonder in the wilderness. He was such a placid beast that someone had likely neglected to keep him secured and so Windkicker had just as placidly slipped away to find his lost companion. He had proven himself to be as fiercely loyal as he was clever, and the cowboy had come close to tears when he saw him again. There hadn't been any real chance to take the animal out since their reunion, and both man and beast seemed more than ready to ride together again. Besides the somber duty that lay ahead, both man and beast had suffered from cabin fever while remaining in hiding as they had been.

Scott and Allen waited until just after dusk to load up their horses with lanterns, rope, and a pair of canvas sacks to wrap the remains in. It was a somber and wordless ride, intentionally skirting any inhabited places in favor of the complete cover of darkness. Grim determination made the miles pass quickly by and soon the cowboy and his soldier companion found themselves staring into the gaping maw of the well they had so proudly dug what must have been a thousand years ago.

One quiet evening earlier in the week, the cowboy had explained to Allen about the vision he had had when his eyes first fell on the engraved ring of stones around the well. The soldier listened patiently, but had no real explanation to offer that wouldn't have sounded any less crazy than what the cowboy claimed to have envisioned. The two men could not guess if the structure those stones had originally comprised had been intended to call the creatures from whatever distant darkness had vomited them forth or to keep them trapped in the caverns below. Regardless, it was a relief that solemn night when their lantern light fell across a rough layer of mortar rather than the mysterious markings and the troubling sensations they evoked.

Wayne's rope remained as securely tied as it had been in the moment he had descended to unwittingly meet both the cowboy and his ultimate fate. It seemed fitting that the two men use it to bring the ranch hand home again.

"You sure he's down there?" Allen asked, his practiced voice cool and with no sign of the torrent of emotions that must have been flooding through him.

"I only wish he weren't," the cowboy confirmed.

The rope was thick and sturdy, though both of the men discovered that not being at their physical peaks made the climb a good deal more difficult than expected. They were slick with sweat when they reached the bottom and the cowboy had to rest for a full minute before his hands felt steady enough to light the lantern.

"It's going to be holy hell trying to get back out," Allen observed, and the cowboy grunted his agreement. "How did you climb out with Lizzy? Did you tie her to your back? Haul her up after you?"

Scott shook his head as he turned his attention to the second light. "I don't rightly remember. All I get is bits and pieces when I try to think back on that day and, to be honest," the cowboy paused as if not sure how to continue, "I guess I just try not to think back on it too much."

"I can relate," Allen said as he accepted his lantern and held it up to survey the area. It only took a minute for him to feel satisfied that he had his bearings straight. "Lead on, cowboy."

As before, time lost any meaning as they made their way forward, as if the bowels of the earth swallowed the passing minutes the way they seemed to feast upon the flickering glow of the lanterns. The going was slow and unpleasant, perhaps more so because of the grim duty the two men were intent upon performing. Eventually, however, they found the cavern and, with handkerchiefs tied firmly across their noses, set to their grisly task.

The cowboy thanked the powers that be that Wayne's body was in no worse condition than it was. The two halves were puffed and slimy with decay, but they showed no sign that animals had been at them and they slid easily into separate sacks. As horrible as it was to admit, it would be much easier for the two men to carry him home that way.

With that work finished, they did a quick survey of the area but, other than dark stains and splatters on the sand colored rock, there was no sign of the terrible thing that had once laid there in wait. There was a slight temptation to press further into the cavern to see if the monstrosity might still be alive and trying to mend itself, but a short and jarring tremor that suddenly ran through the ground warned the two men that they were likely already pressing their luck as far as it would go.

Another equally unsettling possibility for the missing remains was that yet another of the things had come to claim the body of its own, just as the cowboy and soldier were doing at that moment. If that was the case, whatever truce that might have existed to allow the two men their safe passage was likely a weak and very short-lived one. Haste was made and the grim task concluded as quickly as possible.

The two companions reached the surface again more exhausted than they could have imagined possible. Only a few minutes after leaving the fateful cavern, they had experienced an unexpected and very unwelcome surprise when Wayne's remains began to soak through the burlap of the sacks and their efforts to keep themselves free of the putrid liquid had proven both futile and tiring. More than once they wished they had thought to bring a pole to tie the sacks to, but neither of the men had really wanted to think too hard about the logistics of their gloomy task in enough detail to have planned very well in advance.

At first the horses shied away from the grimly determined men and their accompanying odor, but eventually allowed themselves to be mounted and before long Jesse's humble abode appeared on the horizon. Daylight was still many hours away but the cowboy and the soldier reached deep into themselves and found the strength to dig.

Six feet would have been asking too much, but the two men managed to clear out a reasonable trench and lay Wayne in a friendly piece of earth with as much dignity as the circumstances would allow. Dawn was just cracking over the horizon as they laid their shoves down and looked down at their night's work.

"Why God would take a good man like Wayne from this world and leave an old warhorse like me behind," Allen began, but the rough spoken soldier couldn't think of any appropriate words to finish the thought.

"I will always be grateful that he was there for me that day," the cowboy added. "He saved my life—probably Lizzy's, too."

Allen looked at his companion curiously. When the cowboy had given his account of the events of that terrible day, he had never mentioned Wayne having been more than a friendly voice in the darkness. The ranch hand had been a good and loyal friend, certainly, but that wasn't the same as saving a man's life. Perhaps it was just a case of glorifying the dead—giving them credit they didn't quite deserve because it somehow seemed to give their death more meaning.

"I'm going to tell you something," the cowboy continued, "and I just want you to listen." When no reply came, he said, "I told you that after Wayne died, I just closed my eyes and fired at the black thing. I said that it was just a steady hand and dumb luck that I scored the hits that I did." He paused for a moment. "I don't believe that is entirely true."

Allen grunted that he was still listening.

"You see, I do remember one thing from my time bringing Lizzy back to your Ma's house. I was stumbling along, not even knowing if she was even still alive, when she spoke to me in such a weak voice that I thought that she might have been dreaming."

The cowboy swallowed hard. "'Where's Wayne?' she asked, and I explained that he was gone. Then she asked me, 'Gone to where?' and I just didn't have it in me to tell her any more than that. It wasn't until later that I realized that she had never really met Wayne. Sure, she would

300

have seen him when we broke bread at Bixby's place, but there were a good number of fellows there and I don't remember any of them giving a proper introduction. You know, all of them liked to fawn over a cute little girl at the table, too."

There was a long pause before he continued. "Anyway, a few days later, when I was keeping watch by her bed, Lizzy woke up and asked me again where Wayne was, and I finally had to explain how he had been killed almost the very minute we had found her. I tried to paint him as a kind of hero, someone she should remember in her heart, but somehow she just couldn't seem to accept what I had to say.

"'That ain't so,' she insisted to me, and so I asked her why she thought that. You know what she said? She said she had seen him, Allen. She had *seen* him, so he couldn't be dead."

"Of course she saw him," the soldier answered. "Wayne was the one who found her in the first place. You said so yourself."

The cowboy shook his head, "I don't think she remembers that part. She weren't awake when Wayne leaned down to check on her, not even a little. What Lizzy said is that she remembers seeing me standing over her with my eyes closed, firing at something and that Wayne was standing behind me, keeping my arm steady. She also said she saw him help me climb back up the well when it looked like I weren't going to make it, hauling the rope up or some such thing."

The cowboy let out a long sigh. "I didn't have no answer for her when I heard that, but I explained as best I could that, no matter what she thought she saw, Wayne was really gone now, probably in the same hereafter with her folks, and not coming back. She didn't argue with me no more after that, of course, but I could see in her eyes that she weren't fully convinced by my words neither."

"Just some little girl's fancy," Allen explained calmly. "After all she's been through, it's no wonder if her little mind ain't painted the pictures she wants to see."

There was a pause as the two men continued to stand side by side over the grave of a cousin and a friend. A light breeze blew by, sending a few dried leaves skittering across the freshly packed earth.

"You don't believe that," Scott replied. It wasn't a question.

"No," the soldier admitted.

Dark Rivers

Epilogue

Precious moisture had begun to bead and trickle down the cowboy's neck well before he had even reached the saloon doors. Of course, it wasn't the first time.

Whether it was the grace of God or just a thick skin, the horrors the cowboy once faced had not broken him. Instead, they'd made him hard—hard enough to push on through the heat and the doubt and to a new, darker way of understanding the world. He was not the same man he had been the last time he had found himself stopping for water in a backwater saloon.

The cowboy had been making his way north and east for the better part of a month, careful to avoid people whenever he could, and tending to his and Windkicker's needs as best the land and his meager supply of rations would allow. Finally, however, his provisions had reached their end and he could not safely count on foraging to see him through another day. The dull and battered silver dollar Allen had pressed into his hand on the day the cowboy

303

left the little ranch wouldn't buy much, but the dry-mouthed drifter didn't figure that anybody in that dusty strip of nowhere was going to give him the chance to sing for his supper.

A few careful questions to a pair of bored locals lounging in the shade by the hitching post had revealed that no one in that town had ever heard of Drum Hollow, let alone of any troubles they might be having in those parts. The cowboy could not even be sure if the town was still there, seeing as how much trouble it had been securing a safe source of water, despite all of the thankless effort and sacrifice made to that end. Still, it seemed the wiser course to ask questions first to avoid catching a bullet later.

The saloon, as it turned out, doubled as a general store and the proprietor's suspicious gaze melted into a greasy smile when he saw that the drifter who had just wandered in planned to pay for his cornmeal and beans with silver instead of promises. "I'll fill your canteen if you like," the man offered after all of the goods were packaged and paid for.

"How much?" the cowboy asked with a frown.

"For water?" The barkeep barked out a laugh. "On the house, my friend. On the house."

While the cowboy waited for the man to return, a curious patron wandered over and addressed him from a cautious distance. "You know how to use that thing?" he asked and nodded towards the pistol at the cowboy's hip.

"Who's asking?" the nameless drifter replied.

"Just a man with a problem that a bullet or two might fix," the man explained in an educated voice. He stood a good hand shorter than the cowboy and his moth-eaten suit was covered with the dust of long days on the road. "I ain't promising to make you rich, course, but I can make it worth your time." The little man smiled through a row of yellowed teeth. "You see, I been out looking for a man just like you."

"I don't kill folks for money," the drifter explained curtly, turning back to the counter to gather his rations. It never ceased to amaze him how some folks seem to think anyone with a side arm was either a sheriff or an outlaw, as if they were all living inside the cover of the copy of *Bootstraps and Blood* that was waiting in the cowboy's saddlebag.

"It ain't exactly folks I need killing," the stranger continued, a slight edge of desperation creeping into his voice.

The cowboy turned and faced the man again. The drifter now looked ten years older than his true age, and a short-cropped black beard added a certain fierceness to his visage. Along his forearms were rows of fresh scars, as if he had recently been in a hell of a knife fight and he stood there in his dusty poncho and boots as if he was waiting for some unavoidable fight that might start up at any moment. He really wasn't a cowboy anymore, it seemed. He was a gunslinger, and the man in the dusty suit had recognized it as soon as the trail-worn wanderer had pushed his way through the swinging doors. Maybe life was more like a penny dreadful than the drifter wanted to admit.

The little man took an involuntary step back from the cold gaze of the gun-toting wanderer and fidgeted with the bowler he held in front of him. "It's not me making the request—not really. You see, I represent a man with a problem."

"A killing kind of problem?" the gunslinger asked from behind his stony gaze.

"He's got trouble with," the man hesitated for a moment, as if he was trying to find a delicate way of explaining the problem, "coyotes."

"Coyotes?"

"Or something," the little man admitted.

The gunslinger's lips spread into a thin but knowing smile. "I'm listening."

About the Author

Eric Kerkove is an English teacher and Iowa native. In his free time he enjoys writing, illustrating, and walking any dogs that will put up with him.

© Eric Kerkove

www.ingramcontent.com/pod-product-compliance
Lightning Source LLC
Chambersburg PA
CBHW032208190626
46810CB00019B/2174